KU-317-611

THE BILLIONAIRE FROM HER PAST

BY

LEAH ASHTON

ST. HELENS
COMMUNITY
LIBRARIES

ACC. No. F16

CLASS No.

MILLS
BOON

All rights reserved including the right of reproduction
in whole or in part in any form. This edition is published
by arrangement with Harlequin Books S.A.

This is a work of fiction. Names, characters, places,
locations and incidents are purely fictional and bear
no relationship to any real life individuals, living or
dead, or to any actual places, business establishments,
locations, events or incidents. Any resemblance is entirely
coincidental.

This book is sold subject to the condition that it shall not,
by way of trade or otherwise, be lent, resold, hired out
or otherwise circulated without the prior consent of the
publisher in any form of binding or cover other than that
in which it is published and without a similar condition
including this condition being imposed on the subsequent
purchaser.

® and TM are trademarks owned and used by the
trademark owner and/or its licensee. Trademarks
marked with ® are registered with the United Kingdom
Patent Office and/or the Office for Harmonisation in the
Internal Market and in other countries.

First published in Great Britain 2016
By Mills & Boon, an imprint of HarperCollins*Publishers*
1 London Bridge Street, London, SE1 9GF

Large Print edition 2017

© 2016 Leah Ashton

ISBN: 978-0-263-07053-8

Our policy is to use papers that are natural, renewable
and recyclable products and made from wood grown
in sustainable forests. The logging and manufacturing
processes conform to the legal environmental regulations
of the country of origin.

Printed and bound in Great Britain
by CPI Antony Rowe, Chippenham, Wiltshire

THE BILLIONAIRE
FROM HER PAST

For my Dad, Jeff.

Whether it be for a tennis match, dressage test, job interview or career decision, you have always supported me with your wisdom, your positivity, your love—and your ability to reverse a horse-float. Thank you for always being there for me. I love you. Go Freo!

PROLOGUE

PURPLE.

That was what Mila Molyneux remembered.

And bubblegum-pink. Crocodile-green. Little-boy-blue.

So many colours: primary and pastels, and in stripes and polka dots. Everywhere. On party dresses, balloons and pointed party hats. Or scrunched and forgotten in the mountains of desperately ripped and dismissed wrapping paper that wafted across the lawn.

A rainbow of happy, excited eight-year-olds beneath a perfect Perth sky.

But Stephanie had definitely worn purple to her birthday party all those years ago. Purple tights, purple dress and glittering purple cowboy boots.

Mila remembered how excited her best friend had been that day. She remembered how excited she'd been, too—what eight-year-old girl wasn't excited by a birthday party? It had been years before their dreary Gothic black high school days, so Mila guessed she'd been wearing some shade of red—her favourite colour—but that detail of her memories had faded. As had the memory of what Seb had worn, but he'd been there, too. Three friends, neighbours all in a row, although back then Seb had most definitely still had 'boy germs'.

But that had changed later.

As had Stephanie's backyard.

Today there were no balloons in Mr and Mrs van Berlo's garden. No patchwork of forgotten wrapping paper. No mountain of presents or shrieking of excited children.

And definitely no purple, nor even the tiniest hint of a rainbow.

Instead the guests wore black as they mingled amongst tall tables topped with elegant white flower arrangements. In this same garden, where Stephanie and Mila had played hide and seek hundreds of times, it just didn't seem real. Didn't seem possible.

But then—none of this did, did it?

'If anyone else tells me how lucky we are to have such *amazing* weather today I'm going to—'

Sebastian Fyfe stood beside her, staring out at the monochrome guests beneath the unseasonably perfect winter sky. His voice was strong and deep, as it always was.

It had been years since they'd spoken face to face. Almost as long since their emails and social media messages had dribbled out into nothing.

'If anyone else tells you how lucky we are to have such *amazing* weather today you're going to nod politely—because you get how no one has a clue what to say to a man at his wife's funeral,' Mila finished for him.

Seb raised his untouched beer in Mila's direction. 'Correct,' he conceded. His tone was as tired as his grey-blue eyes. '*I* don't know what to say at my wife's funeral either. Maybe I should steal their material and start the weather conversation myself.'

Mila managed a small smile. 'Do whatever you have to do to get through this,' she said. 'Personally, I'm just not talking to anybody.'

Even her mother and two sisters were giving her the space she needed. But they stood nearby, in a neat half-circle, just in case she changed her mind.

'Is Ben here?' Seb asked, not really looking at her.

Mila shook her head. 'No,' she said. 'We broke up.'

A few months ago now. Steph had known, but obviously she hadn't passed on the news to Seb.

Not that long ago Mila would've told Seb herself—but things had changed.

For a long while they just stood together silently, Seb was tall and stiff and stoic in his perfectly tailored suit, looking like the successful businessman he was—but it was impossible to ignore the flatness of his expression and the emptiness in his eyes. His dark hair was rumpled—it always was—but today it looked too long, as if he'd missed a haircut. Or two.

A waitress offered canapés, which they both refused. Mila swirled her remaining Shiraz in its glass, but didn't drink.

She desperately wanted to say something. To ask how Seb was—how he *really* was. To wrap her arms around him and hold on tight. To cry tears for Stephanie that only Seb could understand. But it had been too long since their friendship had been like that.

It had been six years since Seb and Stephanie had moved to London, and maybe they should have expected things to change with so much distance between them.

'Did Steph—?' Seb began, then stopped.

'Did she what?'

He turned to meet Mila's gaze. 'Did you know?' he said. 'What she was doing?'

Did you know about the drugs?

Mila shook her head. 'No,' she said.

Something shifted in his eyes. Relief?

'Me either,' he said. 'I hate myself every day for not knowing. But it helps—in a way—that she hid it from you, too.'

Mila blinked, confused. 'I wouldn't say she *hid* it from me, Seb,' she said gently, not really wanting to disagree with him on a day like today, but also knowing he deserved her honesty. 'The last time I spoke to Steph was her birthday.' Almost six months ago. 'And we weren't really talking regularly before that. Not for a long time.'

Seb's expression hardened. 'But you're her best friend.'

Mila nodded. 'Of course. It's just...'

'You should've been there for her.'

His words were clipped and brutal. His abrupt anger—evident in every line of his face and posture—shocked her.

'Seb, Steph always knew I was there for her, but our lives were so different. We were both busy...'

It sounded as awful and lame an excuse as it was. Mila knew it. Seb knew it.

Maybe everything had changed when they'd moved to London. Maybe it had been earlier. Not that it *really* mattered. No matter how rarely they'd spoken recently, Stephanie had been her Best Friend. A proper noun, with capital letters. Always and for ever.

Until death do us part.

Tears prickled, threatened.

She looked at Seb through blurry eyes. The sunlight was still inappropriately glorious, dappling Seb's shoulders through the trees. He was angry, but not with her. Or at least not *just* with her. She knew him well enough, even now, to know that he was simply *angry*. With everything.

So she wasn't going to try to defend herself with words she didn't even believe. Instead she could only attempt to turn back the clock—to be the type of friend none of them had been to each other for this past half decade and more.

She reached for him, laying her hand on his arm. 'Seb—if I can do anything...'

He shrugged, dislodging her hand. His gaze remained unyielding. 'Now you just sound like all the others. You've just skipped the bit about the weather.'

And as he walked away her tears trickled free.

CHAPTER ONE

Eighteen months later

MILA TOOK A step backwards and crossed her arms as she surveyed the sea of figurines before her.

Fresh from the kiln, the small army of dragons and other mythical creatures stood in neat rows, their colourful glazes reflecting the last of the sun filtering through the single window in the back room of Mila's pottery workshop.

There was a red dragon with only three legs. A beautifully wonky centaur. A winged beast with dramatically disproportionate wings.

Plus many other creations that Mila now knew she must wait for the children in her class to describe.

It had only taken one offended ten-year-old for Mila to learn that it was best *not* to mention the name of the creation she was complimenting. Now she went with, *That is amazing!* Rather than: *What an amazing tiger!* Because, as it turned out, sometimes what appeared to be a *tiger* was actually a zebra.

Whoops.

But here she was, surveying the results of her beginners' class for primary school age children—a new venture for Mila's Nest—and, to her, the table of imperfect sculptures was absolutely beautiful. She couldn't wait for the kids' reactions when they saw their creatures dressed in their brilliant glazes—such a change from the muted colours they'd worn prior to being fired in the kiln.

A tinkling bell signalled that someone had entered the shop. Mila's gaze darted to the oversized clock on the wall—it was well after five, but she'd forgotten to put up her *'Closed'* sign.

With a sigh, Mila stepped out of her workshop. Mila's Nest was one of a small group of four double-storey terrace-style shops on a busy Claremont Street, each with living accommodation upstairs. Mila had split the downstairs area into two: a small shop near the street, and a larger workshop behind, where she ran her pottery classes.

The shop displayed Mila's own work, which tended towards usable objects—vases, platters, bowls, jugs and the like. Mila had always been interested in making the functional beautiful and the mundane unique.

The man who'd entered her shop stood with his back towards her, perusing the display in her shop window. He was tall, and dressed as if he'd just walked off a building site, with steel-capped boots, sturdy-looking knee-length shorts and a plaster-dusted shirt covering his broad shoulders.

He must have come from the shop next door. Vacant for years, it had been on the verge of collapse, and Mila had been seriously relieved when its renovation had begun only a week or so ago. Even teaching above the shriek of power tools, hammering and banging had been preferable to the potential risk of her own little shop being damaged by its derelict neighbour.

The man picked up a small decorative bowl, cradling it carefully in the palm of one large hand.

'That piece has a lustre glaze,' Mila said, stepping closer so she could trace a finger across the layered metallic design. 'If you're after something larger, I have—'

But by now Mila's gaze had travelled from the workman's strong hands to his face. His extremely familiar and completely unexpected face.

'Seb!' she said on a gasp, her hands flying to her mouth in surprise.

Unfortunately her fingers momentarily caught on the rim of the tiny bowl and it crashed to the jarrah floor, immediately shattering into a myriad of blue and silver pieces.

'Dammit!' Mila said, dropping to her knees.

Seb swore under his breath, and dropped to his haunches beside her. 'Sorry,' he said, inadequately.

This wasn't the way he'd planned for things to go.

Mila looked up, meeting his gaze through her brunette curls. Her hair was shorter than it had been at the funeral and it suited her, making her big blue eyes appear even larger and highlighting the famous cheekbones she'd inherited from her movie star father.

'It wasn't your fault,' she said. 'You just surprised me'.

She piled the largest pieces of the bowl into a small heap, then stood and strode over to the shop's front door, flipping the red and white sign to *'Closed'*. When she turned back to face him she'd crossed her arms in front of the paint-splattered apron she wore.

Her expression had shifted, too. He'd thought, just for a second, that maybe she was glad to see him. But, no, that moment had gone.

'Yes?' she prompted.

He had a speech planned, of sorts. An explanation of why he'd hadn't returned her many phone calls, or her emails, or her social media messages in the months after Steph's funeral—before she'd clearly given up on ever receiving a response.

It wasn't a very good speech, or a good explanation.

Explaining something that he didn't really understand was difficult, he'd discovered.

'I stuffed up,' he said, finally. Short and to the point.

Mila raised her eyebrows, but he could see some of the tension leave her shoulders. Not all of it, though.

'I wasn't contacting you to make myself feel better, like you said,' Mila said. 'Or out of guilt.' Another pause. 'I was worried about you.'

Ah. Yes, he had replied to one email. He remembered typing it, with angry, careless keystrokes. He didn't remember the content—he didn't want to. It wouldn't have been nice. It would have been cruel.

'I wasn't in a good place,' he said.

Mila nodded. 'I know. I wish you'd let me be there for you. Steph was my best friend, but she was your *wife*. I can't imagine how difficult this has been for you.'

She stepped towards him now, reaching out a hand before letting it drop away against her hip, not having touched him at all. He realised, belatedly, that she wasn't angry with him. That he'd misinterpreted the narrowing of her eyes, the tension in her muscles...

She was guarded, not angry. As if she was protecting herself.

He'd known he'd hurt her at the funeral. Not straight away—it had taken months for his brain to function properly again—but eventually. And she was still hurt, now.

That was difficult for Seb to acknowledge. The Mila he knew was always so together. So tough. So assured. She didn't sweat the small things. Didn't put up with nonsense.

But he'd hurt her—and he was supposed to be her friend. Once he'd been one of her closest friends—and the last person in the world who would want to cause her pain. And yet he had. He didn't like that at all.

'You didn't stuff up,' she said after a long silence. 'I mean, I don't think there are really rules in this situation. When a man loses his wife. But I think lashing out occasionally is allowed.' She shrugged. 'I'm a big girl. I can deal with it.'

She was being too kind, too understanding. 'I can still apologise,' he said. 'That's why I'm here. To say sorry. For what I said at the funeral and for everything afterwards. We both lost Steph. I should've been there for you, too. I should've been a better friend.'

He could see her ready to argue again, to attempt to absolve him of all guilt—but he didn't want that. And maybe she understood.

'Okay.'

But he could see she wasn't entirely comfortable.

'I accept your apology. But only if you promise not to send any more mean emails. Deal?'

There it was—the spark in her gaze. The sparkle he remembered from the strong, cheeky, stubborn teenage version of Mila. And the strong, cheeky, stubborn early-twenty-something version, too.

'Deal,' he said, with a relieved smile.

She was twenty-nine, now. A year younger than Seb. She'd matured and lost that lanky teenage look, but she was still very much the Mila Molyneux who featured in so many of his childhood memories. He'd lived two houses down from her in their exclusive Peppermint Grove neighbourhood—although at first they'd had no idea of their privileged upbringing. All the three of them—Steph, Mila and Seb—had cared about was their next adventure. Building forts, riding their bikes, clandestine trips to the shops for overstuffed bags of lollies... And then, once they were older, they'd somehow maintained their friendship despite being split into separate gender-specific high schools. All three had studied together, hung out together. Had fun.

Mila had even been the first girl he'd kissed.

He hadn't thought about that in years. It had, it turned out, been a disaster. He'd misread the situation, embarrassed them both.

Mila was looking at him curiously.

'So, any chance of a tour?' he asked, dragging himself back into the present.

Mila shook her head firmly. 'Not until you tell me why on earth you're wearing *that*,' she said, with a pointed look at his work clothes.

Seb grinned. 'Ah,' he said. 'Long story. How about you give me the tour of your shop first? Then I'll give you a tour of next door and explain.'

'Nope,' Mila said firmly. 'You're giving me your tour first—because I *need* to find out how an international IT consultant has ended up renovating the shop next door.'

'Well,' Seb said, smiling fully now, 'that's kind of all your fault, Mila.'

'*My* fault?' Mila said, tapping her chest as if to confirm who he was referring to.

'Most definitely,' he said. Then he grabbed her

hand and tugged her towards her front door. 'Come on, then.'

And, for one of the very few times he could remember, Mila Molyneux looked less than in control of a situation.

Seb decided he liked that.

CHAPTER TWO

SEB'S HAND FELT DIFFERENT.

Not rough, or anything. Just… Mila didn't know how to describe it. Tougher? As if this utterly unexpected transformation from brilliant IT geek into rugged workman had not happened recently.

But then—how did she even *know* it felt different? How long had it been since he'd held her hand? Or even touched her?

Years.

For ever.

She gave her head a little shake as Seb led her through the entrance of the shop next door. This was just silly. She'd let go of thinking about Seb's touch years ago—or reacting in any way. She wasn't about to start again now.

Especially not now.

'I promise, Steph, I don't like *him, like him. It's okay.'*

Thirteen-year-old Mila had managed a wide

smile, even if her gaze hadn't quite met her best friend's.

They'd sat cross-legged on Steph's bed, a small mountain of rented VHS tapes between them, awaiting their planned sleepover movie marathon.

'Are you sure?' Steph had asked. *'Because—'*

'Yes!' Mila had said emphatically. *'He's just my friend. I don't have like...romantic feelings for him. I never have and I never will. I promise...'*

He'd dropped her hand now, anyway, oblivious. He'd taken a few steps into the gutted shop and now spread his arms out wide to encompass the cavernous double-height space, pivoting to look at her expectantly.

Mila needed a moment to take it all in. To take *Seb* in.

It had been more than six months since his email—since he'd so unequivocally told Mila never to contact him again. He'd then blocked her and unfollowed her on all social media. Set all of his accounts to private.

Effectively, he'd erased himself from Mila's life. And, on the other side of the world, she'd been helpless to do one thing about it.

Rationally, she'd understood that he was in a dark place, and that his behaviour was not about *her*. That he wasn't deliberately trying to hurt *her*. But it had still hurt.

So she hadn't expected to see Seb again. At least, not like this. Certainly not dressed like a builder, proudly showing off the elderly, crumbling building next door.

She wasn't sure how she felt about it. After shock, her immediate reaction on seeing Seb had been joy—maybe a Pavlovian reaction to seeing her once-so-close childhood friend. But now she wasn't so sure. She felt confused. And cautious, too. His apology, his earnestness… It was such a contrast to what she'd believed to be her last ever interaction with Seb Fyfe.

Mila surveyed the dilapidated space. It was the exact external dimensions of her own place, and it was interesting to see how her shop would look without necessities like a staircase or—well, the entire first floor. The walls had been stripped of plaster, leaving bare brick, and there was absolutely no lighting. Now, at dusk, little light pushed through the dirty, cracked shop windows and the open doorway behind her.

Basically—it was a big, dark, empty, filthy room.

'Well,' she began, 'I may need to hear a bit more of your plans before I can be appropriately impressed.'

Seb's lips quirked upwards. God, it was so *weird*, seeing her old friend dressed like this. He'd always had lovely shoulders, but now they were muscled. And, yes, of course he'd always been unavoidably handsome. But more in a lean, very slightly geeky way—befitting his career in IT consulting and her memories of him tinkering with hard drives and other computer paraphernalia.

Now he looked like a *man*. A proper, grown-up man—not an oversized version of the teenage Seb she remembered. And not even one per cent geek.

Seb had always been self-assured, always had that innate confidence—probably partly because he had enough family money behind him to know it was nearly impossible for him to fail in anything—but mainly, Mila felt, because that was the kind of guy he was. But now there was something more. Something beyond the confidence she recognised. An...*ease*.

And it was an ease he had now, in his tradesman's outfit, that she hadn't even realised he'd lacked in a five-thousand-dollar suit.

'Fair enough. There's not a lot to see just yet.' He pointed to the far wall, where a large poster-sized plan was taped to the bricks. 'The details are there, but really it's nothing too exciting. It'll be fitted out for a fashion retailer I've got lined up—a good fit for the other shops in the terrace.'

'Fashion? So this isn't some new obscure location for Fyfe Technology?'

That was about as far as Mila had got in trying to work out what this was all about. A trendy suburban location for a multinational company with offices across Europe, the US and Australia and an office already in the Perth CBD? It didn't actually make any sense. But then, she was still trying to process Seb's new shoulders...

Another shake of her head—mentally, this time.

'I sold Fyfe,' Seb said simply.

It was so nonchalantly delivered that it took Mila a long moment to comprehend what he'd just told her.

'Pardon me?'

He watched her steadily. 'It was a difficult decision. Dad wasn't happy at first—I mean, in many ways it was still his company, even though he's been retired for years. But eventually he understood where I was coming from. Why I needed to do this.'

Again his arms spread out to take in the building site.

'And *this* is...?'

Seb shrugged. 'To do what you do. Follow my

dreams without just sliding down my family's mountain of money.'

Mila twisted her fingers together, suddenly uncomfortable. 'I don't think anyone should ever use *me* as a good example for anything.'

'Why not?' Seb said. 'You're doing exactly what you want to do—earning your own income and treading your own path. What's not great about that?'

Mila laughed. 'You're skipping the bit where I dropped out of two different universities, at least four different vocational courses, and completely ignored the advice of basically everyone who cares about me.'

'Exactly,' he said, with a truly gorgeous smile. 'And how awesome is *that*?'

Mila ran her hands through her hair. Yes, she was proud of what she'd achieved, and proud that she lived completely independently of her frankly obscene trust fund, but that was her... Seb was... Seb wasn't like that. Seb had taken his family's already successful business and blown it out of the water. He'd expanded Fyfe throughout Europe, stayed one step ahead of new technologies and made a multi-million-dollar empire a multi-*billion*-dollar one.

'I'm confused,' Mila said. 'Steph always told me

how much you loved your work. How excited you were about the company's expansion, about—'

'How I loved my work more than my wife?' he said.

The sudden horrible, harsh words hung in the air between them.

'No,' she said softly. 'She never said that.'

'Not to you,' Seb said.

Mila didn't know what to do with what he'd said. She didn't know what to do with *any* of this. It was all so unexpected, and it had been so long.

This Seb before her was such an odd combination of the boy she'd thought she'd known and this man she barely recognised. The Seb she'd known would never have sold his father's company. But then, the Steph and Seb she'd known had been deliriously happily married. The Steph she'd known would never have taken drugs.

Emotion hung in the air between them.

'What's going on here, Seb?' Mila said, suddenly frustrated. She'd never thought she'd see or hear from Seb again. And now here he was, with unexpected apologies and painful memories. 'Because I don't for a minute believe that your new dream just coincidentally started with the shop next door to mine.'

A small but humourless smile. Then Seb rubbed

his forehead. 'Okay—here's the deal. I sold the company, donated a big chunk of the proceeds to addiction-related charities and then put some aside for the children I have no intention of having—that would require a wife—but my lawyer still insisted I provide for. Then I gave myself a relatively modest loan—' he named an amount that would buy the row of shops many several times over '—which I will pay back once my new venture takes off. And the new venture is a building company. I've started with smaller developments, like this one, although already I'm starting on bigger projects: think entire apartment blocks, maybe office towers one day.'

'So your dream wasn't to play with computers all day but to build skyscrapers?'

Seb shook his head. 'No, my dream was to do exactly what my dad did, but better. Which was the problem. I've spent my whole life deliberately walking in my father's footsteps. I've finally realised that I'm more than that. That I can build a company from the ground up myself.' He paused for a long moment. 'When my acquisitions team recommended I buy this place I didn't know it was next to your shop,' he said. 'But obviously it came up in the research. I should've known, really—I remember the photos you sent through to us when you first bought it.' His lips quirked. 'And that was really what sealed it—'

'So you bought this place because of *me*?'

'No,' Seb said. 'I was always going to buy it for the right price—which I had no problem negotiating.'

There it was—a glimpse of the ruthless businessman Mila remembered. Just this time without the suit.

'The question was whether I'd let you *know* I'd bought it.'

Mila looked again at the building plan. In the corner was the company logo and its name: Heliotrope Construction.

'Steph...' Mila breathed.

'It's not that original,' Seb said. 'But if Steph could call her fashion label Violet, I figured...'

Shades of purple—Steph's favourite colour.

'I like it,' Mila said.

But Seb was moving the conversation along. 'I did consider not being hands-on with this place, to reduce the chances that we'd bump into each other. But that would have been pretty gutless. I've been back in Perth a few months now. I couldn't avoid you for ever.'

Months? Seb's email had been six months ago, and she'd dealt with his rejection then. Even so, it stung to realise he'd been back home for so long. Somehow rejection had hurt less when he was a million miles away.

'I thought about calling. I knew I couldn't email you.' He shoved his hands into his pockets. 'But I had to apologise in person. Buying this place just forced me into action. I'm sorry,' he said again. 'For waiting this long. Since Steph…everything's been messed up. *I've* been messed up…'

'I know,' Mila said. She got it. Or at least some of it. She *did*.

They were both silent for a while. Mila didn't quite know what to think—she'd mentally classified Seb as part of her past. And now here he was—so different—in her present.

'I hope I'm not too late,' Seb said.

'For what?' Mila asked, confused.

'To fix things.' He was watching her steadily, his gaze exploring her face. 'To fix *us*. I'd hoped—'

Maybe he'd seen something in her expression, because for once Seb looked less than completely assured.

'You and Steph were my closest friends. Steph's

gone for ever, but *we* still have each other. I want you in my life again, Mila. If you'll let me.'

Part of Mila wanted to smile and laugh, tell Seb *Of course!* And in so many ways that was the obvious answer.

She'd told him she'd forgiven him for his behaviour amidst his grief. But it had still hurt. A lot. Because she'd certainly had enough rejection in her life—her ex-fiancé being the latest purveyor of rejection. And part of her—the pragmatic side—just wondered what the point actually was.

Had too much time passed? Was it better that their friendship remained a fond memory? Limited only to the occasional catch-up message on social media?

Remembering how she'd felt when he'd held her hand before—the warmth and strength of his fingers and the echoing, unwanted warmth in her belly—Mila thought she definitely knew the answer.

Seb had just lost his wife. And he'd been Steph's *husband.* She had no place considering the breadth of his shoulders or the strength of his hands.

She should keep her distance. Be his friend, but acknowledge that things could never be as they had been. They could never have the connection of their childhood again. It was too complicated. The emotions too intense.

And yet—here he was. Right in front of her. This strange, compelling mix of the cute boy next door and this handsome almost-stranger next door.

Seb must have seen the conflict in her gaze.

'Well,' he said, 'maybe I am too late.'

He was looking straight at her, but his eyes now gave nothing away. Gone was all that emotion, shuttered away.

He really wanted this, Mila realised. This was more than an extended apology or an attempt to make amends. And what was she worried about, anyway? *Really?*

So what if Seb still had the smile that had made her teenage self weak at the knees? She'd dealt with all that years ago. All that messy unrequited love and the whole heap of angst that came with your best friend marrying the first boy you'd fallen in love with. The first boy you'd kissed.

That had been for ever ago.

Today the butterflies in her tummy meant nothing. She was being silly. Right now Seb didn't need her pushing him away for no apparent reason. And—frankly—she didn't really want to push him away. She'd missed him.

'So, do you honestly want a tour of my pottery studio?' she asked.

Seb grinned triumphantly. 'Lead on, Ms Molyneux!'

And of course Mila found herself smiling back.

CHAPTER THREE

'KNOCK, KNOCK!'

The familiar female voice floated through to Mila's shop and was promptly followed by an impatient rattling of the workshop's back door.

'Mila!' Ivy called out. 'Could you hurry, please? I really need to pee.'

Mila grinned as she hurried to greet her sister. Her nephew, Nate, was fast asleep in his pram on the other side of the fly screen, looking exactly as angelic as Ivy said he was *not*.

'Mila? I mean it. I have about fifteen seconds.'

Mila dragged her gaze away from Nate to glance at her sister.

'Maybe ten,' Ivy clarified.

Quickly Mila flicked open the lock, and Ivy sprinted past her to the small powder room in the corner of the workshop used by Mila's students.

'You'll understand one day,' Ivy said as she slammed the toilet door, muttering something about eight-and-a-half-pound babies.

Mila stepped outside, then squatted in front of Nate's pram. There wasn't much space behind Mila's shop—enough for Mila's car, her bins, and a large collection of enthusiastically growing pot plants—all planted in an eclectic mix of pots and vessels that Mila had decided unfit for sale after firing.

Nate held Mila's mail in his chubby fist, collected by Ivy from the letterbox beside the rear courtyard gate. Nate loved junk mail, and he was happily gazing at the lurid colours of a discount store brochure with intent.

She wasn't exactly sure how old Nate was—nine months, maybe? He'd just started crawling, anyway, and talking in musical meaningless tones. He was so beautiful, with long eyelashes that brushed his cheeks and thick, curly blond hair. Both from his father, apparently—although Mila couldn't yet see even a hint of Ivy's hulking SAS soldier husband in delicate, picture-perfect Nate.

Ivy had taken to dropping by regularly—a result of Nate's unwillingness to nap in his cot and, Mila thought, a latent 'big sister' instinct for Ivy to check up on her that had begun just after Steph had died. Originally it had taken the form of daily phone calls from Ivy's office at Molyneux Tower, and had only metamorphosed into actual visits when Nate had come along and so adamantly refused to sleep.

Mila had always been close to both her sisters—but she hadn't seen workaholic Ivy so often since they were kids living at home. And for that Mila figured she owed Nate one.

She leaned in closed to kiss his velvety cheek. 'Nice work, kid.'

'You know what I wish?' Ivy asked a few minutes later, when they were settled with cups of tea on the old wooden church pew that edged one wall of the workshop. 'That I could have banked all those hours of time I wasted over the years so I could have them now. Because, honestly, I don't know how I ever thought I was busy before. This mum stuff is *nuts.*'

Mila raised her eyebrows. 'You didn't have any spare time to bank,' she pointed out. Her big sister had always been the high-flying, high-achieving child in the family—groomed practically from birth to take over the Molyneux mining empire.

Ivy shrugged. 'Maybe.'

Mila smiled. Ivy had never been good at acknowledging her obsession with work.

Her sister leant closer and spoke in a hushed tone. 'This is going to sound terrible, but I'm really enjoying being back at work a few days a week. I can actually get stuff *done*. Yesterday I committed Molyneux Mining to a joint venture project with a British conglomerate. Today I've discovered that Nate no longer likes peas.'

'Don't worry,' Mila said with a grin. 'There isn't actually a Mum Police.'

Ivy sighed. 'Yeah, I know. There is definitely Mum Guilt, though.'

'Hey,' Mila said, catching Ivy's gaze. 'Don't feel bad for enjoying the career you loved before Nate came along. He knows you love him.'

'Words can't describe how much.' A long pause, then a wobbly bottom lip. 'Oh, God, I'm going to blub. Now I can't even blame breastfeeding hormones.'

Mila scooted closer to her sister so she could press her shoulder against Ivy's as they sat together quietly with their now empty teacups.

'Cake?' Mila asked. 'One of my students baked—'

The tinkling sound of the shop door being opened had Mila on her feet, giving a vague gesture towards the small fridge in the workshop kitchenette as she hurried out of the room.

'Good morning—' she began, then stopped. It was Seb. 'Hi!' she said, with a wide smile. Mila still wasn't sure if reconnecting with Seb was a good idea—but she couldn't deny that she was pleased to see him.

Seb lips quirked as he glanced at the forgotten teacup in her hand. 'Busy day?' he teased.

Mila shrugged. 'I've had a flood of online orders this morning, actually, after one of my pieces was used in a feature in the latest *Home + Home* mag.' She'd swallowed her pride over a year ago and accepted her sister April's offer to feature one of her indoor planters on her hugely popular lifestyle blog. The subsequent interest from stylists and interior decorators hadn't abated. 'The store makes up a pretty small amount of my income,' she continued, pointedly, 'leaving plenty of time for guilt-free tea.'

'That's my favourite type of anything.' He grinned. 'And, really? "A pretty small amount"?'

'Eighteen point two-three per cent. Down one point nine per cent from the previous quarter.'

'There you go. Mila and her numbers.'

'I had to be halfway decent at *something* at school, otherwise Mum would've completely disowned me.' She hadn't had much interest in anything other than maths, and had been truly terrible at pretending.

'She probably wouldn't have, you know.' Ivy leant casually against the workshop doorframe, her eyes sparkling with curiosity as she glanced between Mila and Seb. 'Probably.'

A pause, and Mila knew her sister had taken in Seb's unfamiliar work clothes. 'I didn't realise you were visiting Perth. It's good to see you.'

Under better circumstances. It went unsaid, but the fleeting reference to Stephanie still made Mila's heart ache.

'Not visiting,' Seb said. 'Back. For good.'

Those last two words he directed at Mila, and her awful, disloyal heart flipped over.

No. In the same minute her throat constricted at the memory of her friend. She was *not* allowed to get all fluttery about Sebastian. She crossed her arms in front of her chest, but that was completely ineffective. Instead, while Seb filled Ivy in on his new business venture, she deposited her teacup on the counter, then needlessly wiped a cloth over the vases in shades of teal and grey that were silhouetted like a skyline in her shop window.

'Mila?'

She didn't even look up at Seb's voice, instead focusing her attention on a non-existent mark on a blue-green glaze.

'I'm sorry—now isn't really a good time,' she said. Maybe if she appeared suitably busy he'd go away—and so would her inappropriate heart-flipping.

'For what?'

She straightened to face him, once again crossing her arms. Aware that Ivy was watching, Mila didn't really know what to say. What *could* she say? *It's not a good time for me to still be attracted to my best friend's husband?*

Accurate, but never, *ever* to be articulated.

At her continued silence, Seb leant a little closer. That didn't help anything.

'I thought you were okay with us being friends again?'

'I am,' she said. And she was. It wasn't Seb's fault she had faulty hormones—or whatever it was inside her that just *would not quit* when it came to Seb Fyfe.

Seb needed her right now. But she needed space. More time, maybe? To recalibrate to a world where she co-existed with Seb without the fact of his being her best friend's husband to stall any heart-flipping or tingling of skin.

He will always be Steph's husband.

She'd been a terrible friend to Steph for too long. That stopped *now*.

'Do you still play tennis?' she said, a bit more loudly than she would have liked.

'On occasion.'

'Great!' she said, even louder. *Dammit.* 'Let's hire a court later this week. Have a hit.'

This was a genius plan. Physical distance. Smacking of objects.

'Sure…' he said, sounding a little confused.

'Great!' she repeated. *'Great!'*

Then finally he left, with a tinkling of the doorbell, and from Mila a significant sigh of relief.

Ivy marched over, every inch the billionaire businesswoman demanding to know exactly what was going on. But before she could open her mouth a low, sleepy cry reverberated from the workshop.

'Later,' Ivy threw over her shoulder as she jogged back to Nate.

Seemed Mila owed Nate another one: *Nice work, Nate.*

Now she had time to work out something to tell Ivy—to explain whatever her sister had thought she'd witnessed. Because Ivy had never known about Mila's unrequited teenage crush. Nor April, for that matter.

And no one was ever going to find out about this silly adult version either.

Seb propped his shoulder against the front wall of his shop. Inside, the sounds of building activity thumped and buzzed through the open door, and a lanky apprentice chippy carted rubble in white plastic buckets to the large skip that hunkered at the kerb.

His meeting with the foreman had gone well. So well, in fact, that Seb knew it wasn't even close to necessary that he checked in with the man each day. Richard had thirty years' experience and knew exactly what he was doing. He knew more than Seb, actually—although to be perfectly honest that wasn't particularly hard for anyone in the construction industry.

This bothered Seb. He'd known from a very young age that he would one day own his father's company. Just like for Mila's older sister Ivy it had been his destiny, and he'd done everything in his power to be worthy of following in his dad's footsteps.

That had included actually knowing what his staff did.

He'd graduated with honours in his Computer Science degree so he could write code like his developers. Then he'd done an MBA as he'd begun taking over from his father. And he'd attended each and every course before he'd sent his staff — whether it be marketing, customer service, project management or system development. He'd known that he didn't get to stop learning just because he was the boss, and he hadn't been about to waste his team's time on a course he wasn't prepared to do himself.

He hadn't pretended he could do *every* job in his mammoth company—and he hadn't needed to—but he'd figured he should be able to walk into any meeting, at any Fyfe office in the world, and not feel as if his staff were talking in a foreign language.

He still had a long way to go when it came to his new venture.

It bothered him that he didn't know enough about joists and sub-floors and ceiling-fixing and roofing and I-beams and...

In fact, his entire prior experience in the building industry involved demoing the bathroom of the London flat he'd owned with Steph prior to its—outsourced—renovation, a disproportionate interest in power tools for a man who didn't have a shed—or a back garden to put one in—and many good intentions to attend a tiling/carpentry/plastering workshop one day.

He'd always been interested in tools and building things. He'd just funnelled it in a technological direction. Steph had encouraged him to take some time off—to do a weekend course, to paint their home rather than having professional decorators return three separate times to get the flawless finish he'd demanded. But that was the problem with being a work-obsessed perfectionist—he hadn't been about to take time off from Fyfe.

Nothing had been worth that. Certainly not a bit of DIY.

'Not me,' Steph had told him more than once. *'Not even me.'*

Seb drained the last of his coffee, his fingernails digging ever so slightly into the takeaway cup's corrugated cardboard outer shell. He stared at nothing—at the sky, at the passing traffic—and finally at the stencilled company name on the side of the battered skip, letting his gaze lose focus.

He'd read somewhere—or heard, maybe, on a podcast or something—that grief hit you like a wave. At first the waves just kept on pounding. Pounding you down and down, with barely a breath of air before you were sucked back under again. But then, over time, the gaps between the waves would grow. They would still hit just as hard—and be just as shocking—but in between you could begin to breathe. To exist again.

Sometimes you even got better at handling the waves, at bracing yourself and swimming back up to the surface. Not every wave though. Some would always sneak up on you and drown you as brutally as the first.

Every memory of Steph...every reminder of his many mistakes...what he could have done...should have done... It wasn't getting easier.

Seb had discovered that the waves didn't stop coming. He had just got better at swimming.

Footsteps drew his attention back to his surroundings. He looked up to see Mila striding along the footpath, her gaze on the screen of her phone. Her eyes flicked upwards as she approached, and the moment her gaze locked on his it skittered away again.

It was just like yesterday: that same unexpected and suddenly closed expression. He had absolutely no idea why.

But then her gaze swung back, as if she was *really* looking at him now, and her long strides came to a halt in front of him.

'I didn't see you there,' she said.

He had a feeling if she had she would have exited via the rear of her shop. The realisation frustrated him. Why was she keeping her distance?

But now she was studying him carefully, as if attempting to translate what the sum total of his face and posture actually meant.

He pushed away from the wall and rolled his

shoulders back, uncomfortable with whatever Mila might have thought she'd seen.

'Are you okay?'

He nodded sharply, not quite meeting her eyes. 'Of course.'

'You don't look okay,' she said—which shouldn't have surprised him. Mila wasn't one to accept anything at surface value.

She took a step closer, trying to catch his gaze.

He knew he was just being stupid now, but for some reason he just couldn't quite look at her—the knife-edged echo of Steph's remembered words was still yet to be washed out to sea.

She reached out, resting her fingers just above his wrist. Her hand was cool against his sun-warmed skin.

'Last night,' she said, as he focused on the deep red shade of her nail polish, 'do you know what I did? I found that photobook Steph made after our trip to Bali when we were about twenty. Remember? Our first holiday without our parents. We thought we were so grown-up.'

He nodded. They'd gone with a group of his and Steph's friends from uni. Mila had just dropped out of her umpteenth course, but that had been back when she and Steph had done everything together.

There'd never been any question—of course Mila would go with them.

'Do you remember that guy I met? From Melbourne?' She laughed. 'Oh, God. What a loser.' She shook her head. 'Anyway, last night I wanted to *see* Steph—see her happy—with you and…uh… me, of course.'

Her words had become a little faster, and he was finally able to drag his gaze to hers. She must be wearing boots with a heel, as she looked taller than he'd expected—actually, simply closer to him than he'd expected.

'It made me smile,' she said. 'And cry.'

Her hand was still on his arm, but she'd shifted her fingers to grip harder—as if she was desperately holding on.

'What I'm trying to say,' she said, her big blue eyes earnest and unwavering, 'is that I get it. These moments. Minutes. Hours.'

'Days…'

But he stopped himself saying the rest: *weeks, months…* Because he'd realised it wasn't true. Not now.

Mila realised it too—he could tell. They stood there on the street, staring at each other with a strange mix of sadness for the beautiful, smart, funny, flawed Stephanie they so missed and relief that their lives continued onwards.

'Are you okay?' Mila asked again.

He nodded. The ocean had stilled. The wave of grief and guilt and loss had receded.

She still gripped his arm. They both seemed to realise it at the same time. Her touch felt different now. No longer cool or simply comforting. Her fingers loosened, but didn't fall away. She didn't step back—but then neither did he.

Her gaze seemed to flicker slightly, darting about his face to land nowhere in particular.

When they'd been about fifteen, Mila had successfully dragged Steph into her Goth phase. Seb couldn't remember what the actual point of it all had been, but he did remember a lot of depressing music and heavy eyeliner.

'You have incredible eyes,' he said, without thinking.

Those incredible eyes widened—and they *were* incredible...he'd always thought so—and Mila took an abrupt step back, snatched her hand away.

'What?'

He instantly missed her touch—enough that it bothered him. Although he couldn't have explained why.

'I was thinking of all that eye make-up you used

to wear towards the end of high school. I hated it. You look perfect just like this.'

Mila's cheeks might have pinkened—it was hard to tell in the sunlight—but her eyes had definitely narrowed. 'I didn't ask for your approval of my make-up choices.'

He'd stuffed up. There it was—that shuttered, defensive expression.

'That wasn't what I meant. I—'

'Look, I really have to go.' She'd already taken a handful of steps along the footpath.

'See you at tennis?' he said. They'd organised it via text for the following evening.

Mila didn't look back. 'Yes,' she said, sounding about as excited as if he'd reminded her of a dental appointment.

Sebastian tossed his empty coffee cup in the skip, then headed back to the building site. He might not need to be here daily to speak to the project manager, but he could find other ways to make himself useful—ideally in usefulness that involved swinging a sledgehammer.

CHAPTER FOUR

THE VERY LAST glimmers of sun were fading as Mila pulled into the Nedlands Tennis Club car park. A moment after she'd hooked her tennis bag over her shoulder floodlights came on, illuminating the navy blue hard courts and their border of forest-green.

The car park was nearly empty.An elderly-looking sedan with probationary 'P' plates most likely belonged to one of the teenage girls warming up very seriously for a doubles match, while the top-of-the-range blood-red sports utility had to belong to one of the two guys around Mila's age who were laughing as they very casually lobbed a ball back and forth.

Judging by the fluorescent workwear tossed in the tray of the ute, Mila could almost guarantee those guys were wealthy FIFO workers: men—generally—who flew in to work at one of Western Australia's isolated mines in the Pilbara for weeks at a time, living in 'dongas'—basic, transportable single rooms—and then flying out for a week or more off, back home in Perth. It was a brutal, but extremely well-paid lifestyle—providing blue collar workers with incomes unheard of before the mining boom.

Mila could never have done it. She'd visited the Molyneux-owned mines many times in her youth, and while she could appreciate the ancient, spectacular beauty of the Pilbara, the complete isolation somehow got to her. Out there you were over one thousand five hundred kilometres from Perth, and not much closer to anything else.

Ivy loved it—she'd married her new husband there, after all. And April did, too, regularly 'glamping' with her husband in remote Outback locations and posting dreamy, impossibly perfect photos on social media. But Mila always felt that she must be missing some essential Molyneux genes. The mining gene, or the iron ore gene, or even the red dust and boab tree gene.

Because Mila was never going to follow in her big sisters' footsteps. Regardless of her uninterest in her education for all of her childhood and the early part of her twenties, it just wasn't who she was. The industry and the land—that was *everything* to the Molyneux empire... Mila just didn't *fit*.

Seb still hadn't arrived, so Mila leant back against the driver's side of her modest little hatchback, the door still warm from the day's glorious spring sun. The two probable FIFO guys had become more serious, and their banter and laughter was now only between points. She vaguely watched the ball ping between them without really following what was going on.

Mila had long believed that there was a lot more of her father in her than her mother. She even *looked* like Blaine Spencer—except without the blond hair. She definitely—or so she'd been told—had her father's intense blue eyes. *'Eyes that'll make the world fall in love with him'*—that was what a film reviewer had said, in the ancient newspaper cutting that Mila had found in a book years after he'd walked out on them when she was only a toddler.

She'd burnt that review—at an angry sixteen—when her father had once again let her down. Not that it mattered. She could still recall every word.

A car slid into the parking spot directly beside her—a sleek, low, luxury vehicle in the darkest shade of grey. Seb climbed out, turning as he shut the car door to rest his forearms on its roof.

He grinned as he looked at Mila across the gleaming paintwork. 'Ready to be run off your feet?' he asked.

The lights in the car park were dim, leaving his face in both light and shadow. Even so, Mila could *feel* his gaze on her like a physical touch. She shivered as his gaze flicked downwards, taking in her outfit of pale pink tank top and black shorts, and then down again to her white ankle socks and sneakers.

Did his gaze slow on her legs?

She squeezed her eyes shut for a moment. Nope. It did *not*.

Just as he'd definitely meant nothing when he'd said *incredible* and *perfect* yesterday.

Mila forced a laugh. 'Last time I checked I still lead in our head-to-head.'

His laugh was genuine as he reached into his car for his tennis bag. He tossed it over his shoulder as he walked around the car to her. 'That doesn't sound right to me.'

He was dressed casually, all in black: long baggy running shorts and a fitted T-shirt in some type of sporty material. It revealed all sorts of somehow unexpectedly generous muscles: biceps and triceps and trapeziums...

The genius of her idea was now clearly questionable.

'Trust me—' Her voice sounded high and unlike

her own. She cleared her throat. 'Trust me—you know how good I am with numbers.'

He shrugged and smiled again, and the instant warmth that little quirk of his lips triggered was unbelievably frustrating.

Mila strode towards the courts, opening the door within the tall cyclone fence and barely waiting for Seb to step through before walking briskly to the court they'd hired.

To be honest, she didn't remember the exact head-to-head score between them. When they'd started lessons together in primary school Mila had been the stronger player. She probably still was—it was just that eventually Seb had become *actually* stronger than her. And significantly taller.

At some point she'd known exactly how many sets she'd won against Seb—she'd kept a tally all the way through high school and into uni, enjoying their semi-regular matches because, if she was truthful, it had been the one thing she'd done just with Seb. For Steph had been many things, but definitely *not* an athlete.

But somewhere along the line Mila had forgotten her hard-earned leading score against Seb. Now, as she dropped her bag at the side of the net, and then fished out her water, racquet and a skinny can of new tennis balls, she searched her memory for a hint—but there was nothing. She might be leading by one or a hundred—she had no idea.

Like so much that had once been important to her when it came to Sebastian and Stephanie, over time she'd allowed it to become less important. And eventually to fade completely away.

Seb stood on the opposite side of the net, his racquet extended, the strings flat, ready for Mila to place a couple of tennis balls on its surface.

He raised an eyebrow. 'You all right?' he asked.

She nodded firmly. 'Yes,' she said—and she was, she realised. 'But I was thinking…let's wipe our scores. Start with a clean slate.'

She couldn't change the past—and, while it might be complicated, she *did* have this second chance with Seb.

His smile was wide. 'I like the sound of that,' he said.

Mila dropped the tennis balls onto his racquet, then stuffed two in her pockets as she headed for the baseline.

'Although,' he called out as she pivoted to face him, 'it's pretty sad that you can't just admit I was winning.'

And Mila laughed as she smacked a forehand in his direction to start their warm-up.

Maybe this wasn't such a terrible idea, after all.

* * *

This had been a *terrible* idea.

'Three-love,' Mila announced gleefully as they changed ends. Her eyes sparkled beneath the floodlights as they crossed paths at the net.

From now on all efforts related to repairing his friendship with Mila would definitely require more clothing.

How had he ever forgotten those legs? They went on and on...

Well, no, he hadn't forgotten them. He was human, after all. He hadn't married Stephanie and then instantly become blind to beautiful women. Certainly not to Mila. But before it had been an objective realisation: *Mila Molyneux has rather nice legs.* Kind of like: *The sky is blue. I don't like raw tomato. My mum cooks the world's best spaghetti and meatballs.* That type of thing.

Certainly nothing more.

Certainly not this...this *visceral* reaction to the curve of thigh and calf. This tightening in his belly...this heat to his skin. As sudden and as unexpected as a punch to his stomach.

It was his serve. He took a deep breath as he bounced the ball a handful of times before rocking back onto his heel as he tossed the ball high into the night sky.

Thwack.

Ace. Good.

'Fifteen-love.'

But *was* it sudden? This reaction?

He hadn't let himself analyse what he'd said yesterday, or questioned his choice of words. He'd told himself he'd just been speaking the truth when he'd told Mila her eyes were incredible. That she was perfect.

Hadn't he always thought so? Objectively, of course. So why verbalise those facts now? Especially when she'd been standing so close to him. Close enough that it had only been after she'd walked away that he'd realised his heart-rate was decelerating, that his body had registered more than simple comfort in her proximity.

Thwack.

The ball landed so far past the service line that Mila didn't bother calling it. Instead she grinned, catching his eye as she took a couple of steps forward, ready for a less powerful second serve.

Thwack.

He'd hit it even harder than his first serve, his tennis tactics being the furthest thing from his mind.

'Out!' Mila said, as it landed a ball-width too wide of the centreline.

She still hit it back, and he blocked it with his racquet, bouncing it a few times before shoving the ball in his pocket.

'Fifteen-all.'

Mila held up her hand before he went to serve again, to indicate that he should wait. He watched as she fussed with her hair, pushing it behind her ears and sliding in the clips that kept it out of her eyes. There was absolutely nothing provocative about what she was doing—if he ignored the pull of her singlet against her skin as she raised her arms. And the shape of her waist and breasts that the thin material so relentlessly clung to.

Which, despite his best efforts, he could not.

He turned away abruptly, and for the first time in his life smashing his racquet into the unforgiving surface of the court seemed an excellent option. He could almost feel it—the satisfaction of channelling his body into destroying something rather than generating seriously inappropriate thoughts about Mila.

His friend. His *friend*.

Stephanie's *best* friend.

No, he wasn't going to ruin his racquet—just as he would never allow himself to ruin things with Mila. He would not and he could not.

Not much was clear to him any more except two

things: his new business and his need to have Mila back in his life. Platonically. Because even if Mila saw him as more than the once awkward, occasionally pimply teenage nerd who had lived next door—which seemed unlikely—a relationship was not an option anyway.

With Mila or with anyone.

He stepped back to the baseline.

Thwack.

Ace.

'Thirty-fifteen.'

There had been women since Stephanie. Two, to be exact. Meaningless, nothingness. Found in a fog of grief in London bars without even the decency to remember their names. He'd woken up alone and even emptier—so he'd stopped.

It had been months since the last. Almost a year.

Thwack. Thwack. Thwack.

Winner—down the line.

'Forty-fifteen.'

So he'd failed at casual sex and he'd clearly failed at marriage. He could barely remember the last time he'd slept with Stephanie—he'd always been working away, or late. *Too* late. And when he *had* been home there had still been distance between them. He'd fobbed Steph off when she'd attempted to address it. He couldn't remember how many times.

He did remember the shape of her body as she'd slept alone in their bed, her back towards his side. Always.

He'd refused to make time for Steph and he'd stubbornly ignored—or at best minimised—her concerns about their relationship. The lack of communication. The lack of intimacy. Their effectively separate lives.

The concerns of the woman he was supposed to love.

What sort of man did that make him?

A man who hurt the people he loved. A man who shouldn't *do* relationships. A man who'd driven his wife to make catastrophic choices.

Thwack. Thwack. Thwack. Thwack.

Mila had chased his cross-court forehand down and thrown up a high lob. He ran to the net, waiting for the ball to fall and for the opportunity to smash that ball into oblivion. He had his racquet up, ready.

Up, up, up...

Down, down, down...

And then, powered by every single uncomfort-

able, unpleasant, unwanted emotion inside him...
thwack.

It was the perfect smash—right in the corner on the baseline. Mila had no chance to reach it but she tried anyway, stretching her legs and arms and her racquet to their absolute limit.

Then somehow all those outstretched limbs tripped and tangled, and with a terrible hard thump Mila tumbled to the ground, skidding a little on the court's unforgiving surface.

Sebastian was in motion before she'd come to a stop, his feet pounding as he ran to her.

Mila had levered herself so she was sitting. She held up her palms, all red and scratched.

'Ow,' she said simply, with half a smile.

Seb dropped down beside her. 'Are you okay?' It took everything he had not to gather her in his arms. He worriedly ran his gaze over her, searching for any sign of injury.

Mila stretched out both her legs experimentally, then wiggled her ankles in a circle.

'All seems to be in order,' she said, looking up at him.

'Not quite,' he said, and it was impossible to stop himself from reaching out and turning her arm gently, so Mila could see the shallow scratches that tracked their way along the length of her arm. Tiny pinpricks of blood decorated the ugly red lines.

'That looks worse than it feels.'

'You are one tough cookie, Mila Molyneux,' he said.

She smiled—just a little. 'Sometimes.'

Like yesterday, their eyes met. And once again Seb found himself lost in her incredible blue eyes. This time there was no pretending he was being objective, that he was admiring Mila simply as his strong, beautiful friend.

No, the way he felt right now had more in common with his fourteen-year-old self. Like then, his hormones were wreaking havoc on his body, his brain firmly relegated in the pecking order.

He'd forgotten. Forgotten what it was like to look at Mila this way, to see her this way—to *want* her this way. It had been so long.

But how was she looking at *him*? Not with the disgust he'd expected, that he deserved for ogling his *friend*. More like—

A loud whoop from the neighbouring court ended the moment before it had fully formed. Seb looked up. The two young guys had finished their match, and the shorter of the two was completing a victory lap around the net.

Meanwhile Mila had climbed to her feet.

'Three-one,' she said firmly, with not a hint of whatever he might have just seen in her eyes. 'My serve.'

CHAPTER FIVE

MILA'S PHONE VIBRATED quietly beneath the shop counter as she carefully wrapped a customer's purchase in tissue paper.

The older gentleman had bought a quite extravagant salad bowl, with an asymmetrical rim and splashes of luminous cerulean glaze. For his granddaughter, he'd said, who had just moved out of home along with a mountain of the family's hand-me-down everything. *'I want her to have a few special things that are just hers alone.'*

After he'd left, Mila retrieved her phone and propped her hip against the counter. It had been a busy Friday, with a flurry of customers searching for the perfect gift for the weekend. She still had half an hour before Sheri arrived to take over the shop while Mila taught her afternoon classes—and so half an hour before she'd get to eat, as her rumbling tummy reminded her.

Lunch?

The text was from Seb, as she'd expected.

Sure. Pedro's?

Text messages from Seb had become routine in the two weeks since their... Mila didn't even know how to describe it.

Strained? Tense? Awkward?

Charged.

Yes, that was probably the correct word to describe their tennis match.

Fortunately Sebastian seemed equally as determined as she was to pretend nothing *charged* had happened, and instead had determinedly progressed his quest to repair their friendship.

That, it would seem, involved regular deliveries of her favourite coffee —double-shot large flat white—and just a few days ago had escalated to a lunch date.

They'd had lunch at a noisy, crowded, trendy Brazilian café—Pedro's—a short walk from her shop and his building site, and the impossibility of deep conversation or privacy had seemed to suit them both just fine.

Not that Seb showed *any* hint that there was anything more to their friendship than...well, friendship. And a pretty superficial friendship, if Mila was honest. They weren't quite spending their time discussing the weather...but it wasn't much more, either.

At times there was the tiniest suggestion of their old friendship—they'd laugh at each other's slightly off-kilter jokes, or share a look or a smile the way that only very old friends could. But those moments were rare. Mostly there was a subtle tension between them. As if they had more of those close moments either one of them might read more into it. As if maybe their friendly looks would morph into something like what had happened when she'd fallen playing tennis. When she'd seen something in Seb's gaze that had made her insides melt and her skin heat.

And as by unspoken consensus that hadn't been a *good* thing, a slightly tense and superficial friendship was what they had.

Which was good, of course. It meant that once Seb had processed his tumult of grief and guilt and loss their rehashed friendship would drift again. There would be no more tension and no more confusing, conflicting—definitely unwanted—emotions.

And her life would go back to normal.

Her phone rang, vibrating in her hand as it was still on silent. It wasn't a number she recognised.

'Hello?'

'Mila Molyneux?' asked a female voice with a heavy American accent.

Mila's stomach instantly went south. She knew exactly who this was.

'Speaking,' she told her father's personal assistant.

For a moment—a long moment—she considered hanging up. It was exactly what her sisters would do. But then Blaine Spencer wouldn't bother calling *them*, would he? He knew which daughter put up with his lies and broken promises.

'Just put my dad on,' said Mila.

This one. This gutless, hopeful, stupid daughter.

'La-la!'

'*Mila*,' she corrected, as she did every time. 'I'm not three, Dad.'

The age she'd been when he'd left.

'You still are to *me*, darling girl!'

Every muscle in her body tightened just that little bit more.

'Any chance you could call me yourself, one time?' she asked, not bothering to hide her frustration. 'You know—find my name in your contacts, push the call button. It's not difficult.'

'Now, don't be like that, *Mila*, you know how hard I work.'

There it was: The Justification. Mila always cap-italised it in her mind.

Why didn't you call for <insert significant life event>?

But you said you'd come to <insert significant life event>.

And then The Justification.

You know how hard I work.

Or its many variations.

You can't just pass up opportunities in this in-dustry.

Work has been crazy!

This director is a hard-ass. I'm working four-teen-hour days...

But always: *You know I love you, right?*

Right.

'So you've been working hard for the past three months, then?'

She'd done the calculations. In fact, this was pretty good for him. Normally his calls were bi-annual. Maybe that was why she hadn't hung up on him.

'I have, indeed,' he said, either missing or ignor-ing Mila's sarcasm.

To be honest, Mila didn't know him well enough to say which. Maybe that was the problem—she clung to the possibility that he was just thoughtless, not a selfish waste of a father who knew exactly how much pain he caused.

'I've just landed in Sydney for the premiere of my latest.'

He always expected Mila to know everything about him.

'Latest what, Dad?'

'Movie,' he said, all incredulous.

Mila rolled her eyes.

'*Tsunami*. The director's from Perth, so the Australian premiere is over there tomorrow night. I'm doing a few cast interviews in Sydney today, then hopping on a plane tonight. You won't believe it, but I'm booked on a late flight because Serena has no concept of how far away bloody Perth is...'

Blaine Spencer just kept on talking, but Mila wasn't paying attention any more. 'Wait—Dad. You're coming *here*?'

'Seriously, I wouldn't be surprised if she'd booked us a hotel in Melbourne instead of Perth. All the capital cities are the same to her—' He finally registered that Mila had spoken. 'Yes,' he said, as if seeing his daughter for the first time in six years was something totally normal to drop obliquely into conversation. 'Just for the night,' he clarified, because bothering to extend his stay to visit with his daughter would never occur to him.

'Okay...' Mila said—just to say something.

'If you want to catch up you'll have to come to the premiere,' he said. 'I'm doing radio interviews tomorrow morning and then I'll have to sleep most of the day. You know I can never sleep on a plane.'

She didn't. She didn't know him at all.

'So if I can't make it to the premiere I won't see you?'

'No. Sorry, darling. Can't stay this time.'

Here it comes.

'Pre-production has already started on my next. Got to get to work!'

It took Mila another long moment to respond. All the words she wanted to say—to spew at him—teetered on her tongue.

There was nothing unusual about this phone call. The last-minute nature of his invitation, the way he'd somehow shifted the responsibility for them seeing each other onto her, his total lack of awareness or consideration for her own plans for the weekend. Or for her *life*, really.

No, nothing unusual.

If—somehow—Blaine got Ivy's phone number, or April's, and either woman allowed the conversation to continue beyond the time it took to hang up on him, Mila knew how her sisters would respond to what was hardly an invitation.

With a *no*. A very clear, very definite, I'd-rather-scrub-the-toilet-than-waste-my-time-on-you *no*.

They would each be furious with Mila for even considering seeing him. For even answering this phone call.

The little tinkling sound of the doorbell drew Mila's attention away from her father for a moment.

It was Seb. Of course.

He gestured that he'd wait outside, but Mila held up a hand so he'd stay. This wouldn't take long.

'Just get Serena to email me the details,' she said.

'So you'll come?'

And there it was. The reason why she had always been going to go to her father's premiere. That slightest of suggestions that maybe her dad had been worried she'd refuse to see him. The hint that he was genuine about this—that he really *did* want to see his youngest daughter.

After all, why else would he invite her?

Ugh, she should know better.

But she just couldn't stop herself:

'I'll see you tomorrow,' Mila began, but her dad had already handed his phone back to his assistant. Such typical casual thoughtlessness made her shake her head, but smile despite herself.

'Who was that?' Seb asked as he approached the counter.

Behind them, Mila heard the familiar creak and bang of the workshop's back door that heralded Sheri's arrival.

'Dad,' Mila said simply. She'd considered lying to Seb—broken families and deadbeat parents were certainly not *de rigueur* for their superficial conversations of late. But then—it was *Seb*.

Even so, her lips formed a perfectly straight line as she waited for his reaction. Would he be angry that she still spoke to her Dad? The way that Ivy and April were?

Seb knew the whole story. He'd experienced the fall-out of typical Blaine Spencer incidents, he'd listened to many Mila rants, and once—on that terrible sixteenth birthday—let her heavy tears and Gothic eyeliner soak into his T-shirt as she'd clung to him and Steph.

So maybe she'd see pity. Pity for the woman who—at almost thirty—wasn't all that further along in her emotional development than her sixteen-year-old self. At least, not when it came to her father.

He'd be right to be angry, or to pity her. Or both.

Hell. Mila was angry with *herself*. If she was her own friend she'd definitely pity herself, too.

I mean...how pathetic! Keeping that little hopeful wretched flame burning for a dad who doesn't deserve it...

'You ready to go?' he said instead. 'I'm starving.'

Then he smiled. And in that smile there was understanding and acknowledgement of all Seb knew about her relationship with Blaine Spencer. But there was no judgement, no anger. Certainly no pity. Just support and a gorgeous, heavenly Sebastian Fyfe smile.

It was *exactly* what she needed.

As was a lunch, spent window shopping as they walked and ate their Brazilian *choripán* hot dogs, talking about absolutely nothing important.

Until they arrived back at the rear entrance to Mila's shop, where a handful of her students were already chattering loudly inside.

'I'm coming with you,' he said, firmly and abruptly. 'I have no idea where you're meeting him, or what your plans are, but I'm coming. At least until I'm sure that idiot actually turns up to see the daughter he doesn't deserve.'

Mila blinked. 'You are?'

'I am. Text me the details once the selfish moron's assistant sends them.'

Mila found herself laughing rather than arguing—and then Sebastian was walking away, before she had a chance to say anything anyway. Although any argument would have rung hollow. Seb had known she needed him tomorrow night, even if she hadn't.

And right now she didn't care about anything else that might or might not be complicating things between them. She was just glad Seb was here.

'Ivy has instructed me to convey her disapproval,' April said as she opened her front door. 'However, Nate has just vomited all over her, so she's taking him to the doctor instead of telling you personally.'

'Is he okay?' Mila asked as she followed April down her hallway. Her sister lived with her husband in an airy, modern home close to Cottesloe Beach, with heaps of windows and moody, muted artwork on the walls.

'Ivy thinks so. She suspects he's eaten one of the older kid's crayons at playgroup, given his vomit is blue, but she's just making sure.'

'Gross,' Mila said.

'I can't wait,' said April, deadpan.

She and Evan were actively trying for a baby. April even said it like that—'We're actively trying'—if anyone was dense enough to ask that intensely personal question. April said it made it sound as if they were having sex hanging from a chandelier.

They actually *did* have a chandelier—a modern version—and it was under all its sparkling refracted daylight that April had laid out a selection of evening gowns on her dining table.

'Just to be clear,' she said, 'I disapprove as well. He'll make you cry, and he's not worth it.'

That wasn't entirely accurate. Mila hadn't wasted her tears on her father for at least a decade. But she understood what April meant.

'I thought you'd be angrier,' Mila said.

April shrugged. 'You were wise to tell me via text. I got to be angry at you via Evan.'

'I'm sorry.'

'For Evan? Or for going to see Dad?'

'For Evan,' Mila clarified. 'Not for Dad. I *have* to see him. I can't not.'

April tilted her head. Her long blonde hair was piled up in high bun. 'Hmm…I've been there. You'll grow out of it.'

Mila's jaw clenched, but there was no point in arguing. Although she was less than two years younger than April, and five years younger than Ivy, they both definitely suffered from an ingrained belief that they knew best when it came to Mila's life. The fact that they both resented similar behaviour from their mother when it came to *their* lives was utterly lost on them.

Fortunately their mother had long ago given up advising Mila on anything. They'd become much closer since Irene Molyneux had let go of her ill-fitting dreams for her youngest daughter and accepted that Mila would be creating art with earth's natural materials—not mining them.

April was rattling off the names of dress designers, not that any of them were meaningful to Mila. Her eye was drawn to the darkest fabric—a deep, deep navy—a welcome contrast amongst the frothy pastels.

It fitted well, and Mila felt good as she twisted and turned in front of the mirror in April's spare room.

Her sister poked her head inside the door. 'Oh, that's *lovely*,' she breathed, and Mila smiled. 'Can I post a photo to—?'

'*No,*' Mila said, and laughed.

Seb hadn't been upstairs to Mila's apartment before. It was nice. Small—a single open-plan living area—with the kitchen positioned in front of a large window that overlooked the tree-lined street. Mila had muttered something about making himself at home as she'd raced up the stairs ahead of him, her hair still damp around her shoulders and a bathrobe knotted at her waist.

He walked over to the kitchen, running a hand aimlessly along the pale granite countertop. Mila had obviously renovated. The kitchen was simple but modern, sitting comfortably amongst the original wide timber floorboards, tall skirtings and ornate cornices. The wall the apartment shared with his own shop was exposed—a mix of red brick and mortar and patches of artfully remaining patches of plaster—as it was on the floor below. From the ceiling hung a simple black industrial light fitting, and the living area was furnished with mid-century low-line pieces in a style that had recently become fashionable again. But, knowing Mila, the rich tan leather couch and the elegant, spindly dining suite would be the real deal, not replicas. Seb could just imagine Mila busily searching for treasures in some dusty old antique furniture store.

It was almost dark outside, the street light outside the kitchen window already softly lit. He checked his watch.

'We're going to be late,' Mila said, behind him.

Seb pivoted to face her—and whatever he'd been about to say froze on his lips.

Somehow he hadn't thought ahead to this part—to the reality of escorting Mila to her father's film premiere. His focus had been on just *being* there, and nothing else—certainly not on what Mila would wear, or how she might look. Or that it might suddenly—shockingly—as he stood in her kitchen in a charcoal suit, feel like a date.

She wore a dress of navy blue, in some soft, draping material that wrapped around her waist and the curve of her breasts, leaving her shoulders bare and falling straight from her hips. Her hair was different—smooth and sleek and pushed back from her face—so that all the focus was on her brilliant blue eyes and the ruby-red of her lips.

Those brilliant blue eyes met his gaze, steady and sure. 'It's April's,' she said, her hand casually smoothing the fabric against her hip. 'I thought it looked all right.'

'An understatement,' he said, and he didn't miss the hint of a blush that warmed her cheeks, although she didn't look away.

'Thanks,' she said, very matter-of-fact.

Mila was equally businesslike as she located her clutch bag and he ordered a taxi. And as she marched down the steps ahead of him and locked up the shop. Then all the way to the small theatre near the beach which had apparently inspired the film—thankfully without *any* history of apocalyptic tsunamis—and as they approached the red carpet.

It was there that she went still. That her confident stride and chatter spluttered away to nothing.

Parked along the street was a van for each of the local television stations. A large crowd had gathered behind the cameras to watch the arrivals. Blaine Spencer might not be an A-lister, but the large posters flanking the entrance revealed that the movie's star was an up-and-coming Australian actress—famous enough that even Seb had heard of her.

Automatically Seb reached for Mila, aiming to put his hand at her elbow, but she shook him off.

'I'm fine,' she said, very firmly.

They hadn't quite reached the bright lights that lit the red carpet, but Seb could still see well enough to read Mila's expression.

Was she fine? Mila had always been good at relaying her father's latest example of uselessness when they were teenagers. But, looking back now, he realised she'd done so with a large truckload of bravado—she'd been simply telling a story. It was only that one time, when Blaine hadn't turned up at her sixteenth birthday party, that she'd shown any emotion.

He remembered how awkward he'd felt as she'd

sobbed into his shoulder, sure he was being of no help at all, but also certain that he wasn't going anywhere.

He didn't feel all that different now.

Mila raised an eyebrow. 'Really,' she said. 'I'm not going to blubber all over you again. Don't panic.'

His lip quirked upwards. He was not surprised she'd referenced the same memory. 'My shoulder remains available if needed. Both of them, actually.'

'Noted,' she said, smiling now. 'But I'm not an angsty teenager any more. I'm an adult with possibly the most selfishly unreliable parent in history. I know what I'm doing.'

He opened his mouth—before snapping it shut again.

'Then why am I doing it?' she said, reading his mind. 'I suspect when I work that out I'll finally stop answering his calls.'

Seb nodded, even though he didn't really understand. 'So, let's do this?'

Mila's smile had fallen away, and something had shifted in her strong, determined gaze. But still, ever Mila, she straightened her shoulders, and he watched her take a long, deep breath.

'Let's go,' she said.

* * *

Without Ivy, April or her mother by her side, not one of the photographers or reporters along the red carpet recognised Mila as a Molyneux. That suited her just fine—she'd never had any aspirations to embrace the quasi-celebrity that her family name might give her.

Ivy's job meant she had no choice but to network with the rich and famous, and April had always loved that scene—and in recent years had certainly grown her status as a society darling. Both would've been at home on the red carpet, would've known exactly what to say, how to smile, how to pose for photographs.

Although, her father wasn't famous enough that even if an enterprising paparazzo *had* recognised her it would have mattered.

Her mother had never spoken much about Blaine. Mila knew they'd had a whirlwind romance and a turbulent relationship, and that it had been somewhat of a scandal at the time—the billionaire mining heiress and the Hollywood heartthrob. But that had been more than thirty-five years ago. Old news. Plus none of them—not her mother nor her sisters—had ever breathed a word about their fractured relationship with their father to the media. To anyone, really.

Even at that sixteenth birthday party, when against her own judgement she'd agreed to an elaborate, expensive celebration inviting everyone she knew—and many she didn't—the only guests who'd known of her devastation at her father's absence had been Seb and Stephanie.

And even then she hadn't been stupid enough to tell anyone that her father was coming. Even then she'd suspected he'd let her down.

Tonight, she could almost guarantee he would. Yet here she was. Letting that minuscule tendril of hope drag her down a red carpet.

'Sebastian!'

The shout came from within the throng of reporters. Mila glanced up at Seb.

'Must be a famous Sebastian here,' he said, and kept on walking.

'Sebastian Fyfe!'

Now there was no mistake.

'Keep on walking,' Seb said, stepping closer and leaning inwards. 'Tonight isn't about me.'

They were almost at the entrance to the theatre, but were stalled by a group who were posing for photographs: a single woman in a gold-spangled dress flanked by men in matching tuxedos.

'Why?' Mila asked, confused.

'Didn't I tell you I've taken up a career in film?'

he said, with a smile that looked forced. 'In between my building projects, of course.'

The joke fell pancake-flat.

'Give us a photo with your new girl!' that single voice shouted, explaining everything.

'Oh,' Mila said, unnecessarily.

Seb just clenched his jaw.

'Should we explain?' Mila said. 'That we're just friends?'

'It's none of their business,' Seb said, his gaze directed straight ahead, as if he was willing the people blocking their path to move.

'I think we should,' Mila said. 'I don't want anyone to think—'

'What?' Seb said, his voice suddenly harsh. 'That I've moved on? I think it's allowed. I'm sure I've met society's rules about appropriate mourning periods.'

He looked down at her now, his eyes revealing that awful emptiness she remembered from the funeral.

'And, of course,' he continued, 'what everyone thinks is *always* my number one priority.'

'Of course you're allowed to move on,' Mila said, annoyed now. 'You know that's not what I meant.'

Cameras continued to flash ahead of them.

'Look,' he said, '*we* know we're not together.

That we're friends—we've only ever been friends, and will only ever be friends.'

The nonchalantly spoken words shouldn't have landed so heavily, but they did. Heavily enough that Mila flinched.

'That's all that matters,' Seb continued. 'What *we* know. What *we* think. You know that—you've never cared about what anyone else thinks about you.'

That earlier moment had passed, and that emptiness was gone from his gaze. Now he just looked at her curiously.

'You're right,' she said, reminding herself as well. 'I've always thought all this stuff is total nonsense.'

'Exactly,' he said.

Finally the traffic on the red carpet was flowing again, and they quickly put distance between themselves and that lone, determined reporter, making it into the relative calm of the bustling theatre foyer.

'Mila!'

This time the voice came from ahead of them, thick with an American accent.

Seb stepped closer, his shoulder bumping against hers. Without a word she pressed back against him, just for a moment, her bare arm against the subtle texture of his suit. His warmth, his strength.

'In case I forget later,' she said softly, 'thank you.'

He tilted his head in subtle acknowledgement. 'You've got this,' he said.

CHAPTER SIX

SEBASTIAN FIGURED IT was just his luck that a reporter who read the business pages was at the premiere.

Steph had always enjoyed these types of events. As Fyfe Technology had grown they'd found themselves invited to all manner of charity balls, or museum openings or exclusive cocktail evenings. For a long time Seb had enjoyed them too. It had been part of their big move to London, after all—an opportunity to network in international circles both for Seb and also for Steph and her fledgling fashion label.

He could still remember how they'd worked as a team. Stephanie had always been so charming and so beautiful. She'd drawn people to her, in a natural way that Seb had always admired. For Seb, networking had been more of an effort—a successful one, but an effort nonetheless. It had been Steph who was in her element—smart, sexy and cheeky. He remembered how she'd meet his gaze during those interminably pointless conversations that seemed a given at every event—with a subtle quirk to her eyebrow, the barest roll of her eyes…

Or maybe they hadn't been as clever as they'd thought—maybe everyone had seen through the young, ambitious couple in their early twenties with huge dreams, equally huge determination and really no idea how to succeed on a global stage. Not that it really mattered.

Fyfe Technology's growth had been explosive— far greater than Seb had forecast—and Steph's designs had soon been stocked in major department stores. They'd both been so busy, and soon they'd been declining more invitations than they'd accepted.

Or rather Seb had.

'Babe, I told you about this weeks ago. The ball is this *Friday.'*

A shrug.

'I'm sorry. I need to stay on in Berlin. Go without me. I'd just get in the way.'

How many times had he done that?

'So, Seb,' Blaine Spencer asked now, 'what do you do for a living?'

They'd met once before—one year when Blaine *had* visited for Mila's birthday. Unsurprisingly, Mila's dad did not remember him.

They stood in the foyer, where the crowd was beginning to thin as guests filtered into the theatre. Mila stood beside Blaine. She'd gravitated closer to her father as they'd been speaking, and now it was Seb who remained on his own.

Seb watched Mila as he spoke to Blaine. She stood with her standard excellent posture, her chin slightly tilted upwards as she studied her dad. Her expression was completely unreadable.

She looked stunning. Exactly the kind of woman any sensible man would want on his arm as he walked a red carpet.

He had to forcibly drag his gaze away from her, at least pretend he was engaged in this conversation.

What had he told her? *We're friends—we've only ever been friends, and we'll only ever be friends.*

He'd said the words easily—after all he'd been silently shouting them at himself all night.

A woman with a tight ponytail sidled up beside them, talking to Blaine in a low tone before glancing at Mila and Seb.

'Time to take your seats,' she said, with an accent that twanged.

'I'll sit with the cast,' Blaine said, 'But dinner after?'

Mila nodded. 'That would be great,' she said, her tone even.

It wasn't until Blaine had stepped away that Mila met his gaze. Her smile was blinding.

'Seriously—I thought he'd consider this five-minute chat *it*,' she said. 'I'm shocked.'

'Me too.'

Mila grinned. 'Guess I didn't need reinforcements tonight.'

'You never did,' Seb said. 'I'm just here for the free movie.'

Mila shoved him in the shoulder. 'Dork,' she said.

And then they headed into the theatre.

The movie was actually pretty good. Mila rarely watched her father's films. She figured if he couldn't make the time to see her, then she wouldn't bother to see *him*—even if on celluloid. Kind of like her own silent protest. Plus, she knew her dad hated it when he inevitably asked if she'd seen his latest movie and she always said no.

Petty, yes. Immature, yes. But that simply reflected the depths her relationship with her father had reached. Too far gone ever to come back from—or so she'd thought. Tonight had Mila questioning that, and she was glad. Very glad.

At about the time the movie's first skyscraper-sized wave crashed down on the fictional metropolis, Mila nudged Seb with her clutch.

'Guess what's in here,' she whispered.

Seb tilted his head close. Close enough for Mila to feel his breath against her cheek.

'You're kidding me?' he said, before she'd even opened her bag.

She grinned. 'Nope.'

Together they tried, and failed, to silently open their individual bags of brightly coloured sherbet, and then ate them with tiny plastic spoons. Just as they had at many movies, many years ago.

It was a memory from even before he'd started going out with Steph—this was from when they'd walked to the local deli to spend their parents' spare change on bags of lollies before catching the bus to the cinema. All three of them had always each had a bag of sherbet. In their twelve-year-olds' logic it had seemed a very grown-up choice—equally as grown-up as seeing a movie without their parents.

Of course now they were *really* all grown-up. In the darkness, Mila was particularly aware of all-grown-up Seb's size. The way his shoulders seemed to overlap into her space. The way it seemed quite an effort for Seb to keep his legs an acceptable distance from hers. And how they both seemed to have come to the decision that neither of them would use their dividing armrest. Which was uncomfortable—both literally and otherwise. After all, if they were just friends for all eternity what would it matter if their arms accidentally touched?

Fortunately the movie had enough loud bangs and impressive special effects to distract Mila from thinking too much about Seb, or about anything else. At least until after the movie. Then, back in the foyer, she couldn't help but acknowledge—again—how truly excellent he looked in a suit. As she sipped from the Champagne she'd plucked from a passing tray, she decided she was simply being objective.

So objective, in fact, that she told him.

'I didn't say earlier, but you look great. Nice suit.'

Seb's grin was wicked. 'Well,' he said, 'I—'

'Ms Molyneux!'

The voice was unmistakably Blaine's assistant. She hurried over in her sky-high heels, managing to appear both harried and rather bored.

For the first time Mila noticed that even though much of the crowd had dispersed, she hadn't yet spotted Blaine.

'Are we meeting Dad at the restaurant?'

Serena's head-shake was nearly imperceptible. 'No. He sends his apologies. He now has other plans.'

Suddenly Seb was standing right beside her. Close enough that she could lean into him if she needed to.

She didn't.

'I see,' Mila said.

Blaine's assistant waited a beat, as if for a longer message to relay back to Blaine. Eventually the silence *became* that message, and Serena nodded briskly.

Then—just a moment before she went on her efficient, busy way—Serena stepped closer to Mila. 'I'm sorry,' she said, ever so softly.

Then she was gone.

And somehow it was *that* that made the difference. That overloaded the scales, that pushed her over the edge...beyond dealing with this in a reasonable manner. Reasonable because this was not unexpected. None of this was without precedent. *None.*

But rather than just roll her eyes, or make some pithy comment to Seb, Serena's words—Serena's *pity*—made that impossible.

Standing still was no longer an option. Remaining calm was not an option. Pretending she was okay was *not* an option.

Mila didn't remember leaving the theatre, although she *did* remember the sharp, satisfying click of her heels on the footpath as she strode away.

And then the clicking stopped, abruptly, as her feet sank into sand. Beach sand.

She stopped, turning around on the spot to take in where she was.

She stood at the top of a sandy pathway down to the beach. The street lights lit the way somewhat, identifying scrubby plants growing right up to the pine railings.

'Mila!'

It was Seb—and it wasn't the first time he'd called her name, she was certain.

Instead of answering, Mila kicked off her shoes and swung them in her fingers as she headed with purpose towards the beach.

She heard the rustle of Seb removing his own shoes behind her, but didn't slow her pace. He'd follow her—she knew that.

She stopped when the sand became damp beneath her feet. There was enough moonlight that she could watch the small waves stretching towards the empty beach, although it wasn't warm enough that the brush of the water against her skin was anything but extremely cold. She didn't care.

Seb was now beside her, his feet also sinking into the sodden sand.

'Well,' he said, 'that sucks.'

A short laugh burst from Mila's lungs.

'Maybe I should tell myself *I told you so*,' she said. 'Because I did.'

'That doesn't matter.'

'No,' she said. 'My continued delusions when it comes to my father are of absolutely *no* cause for concern.'

'This isn't your mistake,' Seb said. 'Not at all.'

Mila shook her head, staring out at the total blackness of the horizon. 'Of course it is. You've heard the saying, right? Fool me once, shame on you. Fool me twice...' She laughed harshly. 'Fool me a hundred times. Shame on me.'

'Your dad should be ashamed—not you.'

She wrapped her arms around herself, holding tight. 'He should be a lot of things,' Mila said. But, really, she'd only ever wanted him to be one thing.

'He's an idiot for not realising how lucky he is to have you.'

'He doesn't *have* me,' she said. A sharp breeze whipped over the waves, dragging tendrils of her hair out of place. 'I'm done.'

As she said it she realised it was true. Even silly, hopeful Mila had a limit. This, it would seem, was it.

'You sure?' Seb asked.

Mila was so surprised that she finally turned to face him. His dark suit was stark against the pale sand, even in the moonlight. His face was shadowed.

'Why did you give him so many chances?'

Her gaze dropped. His white shirt was bright in the gloom. 'I just said why. I'm delusional—obviously.'

'No, you're not. I'd say you're the least delusional person I know.'

'You don't know me all that well, then. Not any more.'

There was a bit more bite in her words then she'd intended. But it was the truth.

'Maybe,' he conceded. 'But I remember a Mila Molyneux who never let herself be stomped on.'

He was right. Maybe that was the part of her mother she *had* inherited—an accurate radar for all things deceitful and fickle. An intolerance for pretence. It had served her well in business, although clearly it had taken her a little longer to learn to apply it to her relationships. But now she knew exactly how important it was to walk away before she was walked all over.

'My father is my blind spot,' she said. A pause. '*Was*, I mean.'

Her throat felt tight, but she wasn't able to concede to the tears April had forecast.

'Ivy told me that he wasn't all that great a dad when he was around,' Mila said, hoping that talking might help. 'That he wasn't all that interested in us. That he was away a lot. But I was too young when he left. I only remembered the good bits— big bear hugs, stories in bed. I can't remember how often they happened.' She turned back to the ocean again, closing her eyes and focusing on the sensation of the breeze against her cheeks. 'You know, I've asked myself the same question. A hundred times. Ivy and April keep on asking, too.' Another pause. 'Not Mum, though. Maybe she gets it—she seemed to persist with Dad...with Blaine...for a really long time, too.'

It was completely silent except for the soft little rumble of waves.

'It doesn't make any sense. This isn't who I am. I don't like this person. This needy person.' *This vulnerable person.* She *never* let herself feel like this.

'I think it's understandable to wish you had a great dad,' Seb said.

'That's the thing,' Mila said. 'It *was* just a wish. A dream. A fantasy. And when he did deign to involve me in his life it was only an illusion. He doesn't really care about me.'

'No,' Seb agreed. 'I don't think he does.'

Oh, that hurt.

'That's rich,' Mila said, knowing she was being incredibly unfair but not caring. 'Coming from you. Where have *you* been when I needed you?'

'You know how sorry I am for the way I behaved after Steph—'

'You left. You *and* Steph. You got married and— *poof!* You were gone.'

She was directing her anger at the wrong target, but she couldn't stop. She needed an outlet for all this emotion. A target who would actually care.

'You wanted us to stay in Perth for the rest of our lives?' he asked, incredulous.

Mila shook her head. 'No, don't go and be all calm and sensible on me. You had a new and exciting life and you forgot about me.'

'I never forgot about you,' he said.

She never forgot about him, either. Some part of her knew that was the problem.

'I forgot about you,' she said, more quietly now. 'At least I thought I had.'

'I'm sorry—' Seb began.

'No,' she said, quite loudly. 'Don't. I was busy too. I got lazy about staying in touch, too. I know I'm not being fair.'

'Someone told me that it's allowed to be like that sometimes.'

But it was easier when it was other people.

'This was a mistake,' she said abruptly.

'Tonight?' Seb sounded confused.

'No,' she said. 'I mean, yes—of course tonight was always going to be a farce. But I mean...' She faced him, gesturing towards Seb and then herself. '*This*. This is a mistake.'

'Me coming tonight?'

'No, you coming back into my life. I'm sorry, I shouldn't have agreed to it. If we really mattered to each other we would've tried harder to stay in touch. Tonight has just made it clear that some things are better left as memories.'

Memories always benefited from a glorious rose-coloured haze. Reality was complicated.

'You sent me messages for almost a year, Mila. Why would you do that if you thought our friend-ship was a mistake?'

Mila shook her head. 'Because that wasn't about *us*—that was about Steph. That was about my con-cern for you.' She paused, trying to organise her rioting thoughts. 'And, besides, you were on the other side of the world. You weren't supposed to go and buy the shop next door.'

'That's nice. So you were only there for me if I remained at an acceptable distance?'

Yes. No. *No.*

They both knew that wasn't true.

And Mila also knew that she'd *never* expected Seb to come home. Or that if he did she'd feel...

Feel what? She couldn't even describe it.

Off-balance?

Confused?

Uncomfortable?

And worse. Breathless, warm...tingly. Dammit. *Tingly.*

She didn't want this. Not with Seb.

'This isn't a mistake,' Seb said, his voice low but with a hint of something far from calm in his tone.

'Go ahead,' Mila said simply. 'Disagree away. It doesn't change anything. We were always going to end up friendly acquaintances once we'd finished this charade of vaguely awkward lunches and tennis and talking about the weather. Let's just fast-track it.'

'I don't want to talk about the weather with you.'

She'd deliberately referenced his words at the funeral, not caring any more.

'Then what *do* you want from me?' she said.

'Someone to reminisce with about lolly bags at the movies? We can do that on social media. Tag each other in old photos or something.'

'That isn't what I want.'

'We can even make pithy comments and subtle references that no one else on our friends list will understand!' Her voice was gloriously false. 'It will be *so* fun!'

She was done with this now. Her dad was permanently gone from her life, and now Seb was relegated to a category only marginally more intimate.

She had to learn from what had happened with her dad. You couldn't force relationships. And her friendship with Seb—through time and distance and neglect—had been over long ago.

So shouldn't she be feeling good? Relieved?

She refused to think about that.

'That isn't what I want,' Seb repeated.

'I understand,' she said. Mila knew all about not getting what she wanted.

She turned, feeling the sand rough between her toes. She was a few steps into the dry sand beyond the waves when Seb spoke again.

'Is that it?' he said.

Tears threatened again, from nowhere. Desperately unwanted.

'I thought it was pretty clear,' she said, and kept on walking.

'It's not to me,' he said.

If he'd touched her, physically tried to make her stop, she would have shoved him away. But instead he took big strides in the deep sand to overtake her, to stand in her path.

Now she had to walk around him. That was harder than it should have been, even though she knew he'd never stop her.

For a moment it seemed impossible. She just stood there, her eyes trained on the knot of his tie.

'What *do* you want?' she said finally.

'I want you in my life.'

She made herself meet his gaze, annoyed that it was so difficult to do so.

Even in the moonlight she felt too exposed. As if he could see something inside her that even she didn't know about.

'Why?'

'Because you used to be my best friend,' he said.

Mila shook her head. 'Not enough. I'm not living in the past any more.'

No longer would she grasp onto childish hopes and dreams built on snatches of memories. Not with her father, and not with Seb.

'I'm not a substitute for Stephanie,' Mila said suddenly.

'I never thought you were,' Seb said.

Finally she'd made him angry. She'd cracked the veneer of calm he'd been so careful to maintain. Now on the beach. Before on the red carpet. Maybe the whole time he'd been back in her life.

But why did she even want to do that? She had no idea.

'But I am…kind of,' she said gently. Now it was her turn to be calm. 'You lost the woman you loved. I'm part of your same shared memories. It makes sense you'd want to reconnect. And we tried. But it's not working.'

'No,' he said. *'No.'*

'Yes,' Mila said, warming to this theory. 'Don't feel bad about it. It's okay.'

Now she should just walk past him. Or at the very least fish her phone out of her bag and call a taxi. This was over.

But instead she wiggled her toes in the sand. Beneath the relative warmth of the surface the tiny grains were freezing, just a few inches below. Her feet felt heavy, as if the sand was setting around them like concrete.

'Stop it, Mila,' Seb said.

He stepped closer, and it was impossible to move.

'Don't you dare reduce yourself to a variation of someone else.'

Something in the atmosphere had shifted, triggering an uncomfortable tension.

Mila shook her head, as if that would fix it.

Seb stepped closer again.

'Maybe I would be better off as a different variety of Mila,' she said, trying to recall the false levity she'd voiced before. She failed, and simply sounded breathless. 'You know—like a new, improved version? Mila two point zero.'

Now he touched her. His fingers brushed against her wrist, his hand gently circling it, his thumb sliding over her furiously beating pulse.

'You don't have to change a thing.'

Mila could barely think with Seb so close to her. She seemed to be leaning towards him. His tie was still her focus, but it was much closer now.

'My mum thinks I should eat more salad,' she managed.

Seb's laugh was sudden and loud, whipped about in the sea breeze.

'I can accept that,' he said. 'But only if you want to.'

'I will if there's no coriander. That stuff is—'

But her words stopped forming as Seb's hand

shifted, his fingers meshing with hers. She held on tight as she finally lifted her gaze.

The street lights were all behind him, up above the beach, so his face was in almost total darkness. She could just make out the shape of his cheek-bones, the strong line of his nose.

And his mouth.

She definitely knew where his mouth was. It was as if every sensation in her body was focused upon it, as if nothing else existed beyond Seb, Mila, this cloaking darkness...and his mouth.

Her shoes dropped from her fingers to the sand with a soft thud, seemingly releasing her feet from their concrete-like shackles. She stepped closer, because she was helpless to do anything else.

She closed her eyes, trying to gather her thoughts...or something. His breath was warm, soft against her eyelashes.

Snippets of common sense did flitter within her, but with no success. Her body was awash with too many emotions right now for her to pay attention: her father's rejection, the loss of the man she'd always so badly wanted him to be.

Plus the awful emptiness that her attempts to re-move this man right before her from her life had triggered. Even despite her maddening inability to do so.

With all this whirling loss and confusion all Mila knew was that she wanted to feel good. She wanted to feel close to someone—to anyone.

No.

Not anyone. *This* man.

Right now this man felt right. More right than anything else that had happened tonight. That had happened in for ever.

'Mila...'

Oh, God, his voice was low and rough. The voice of a man barely in control.

Seb *wanted* her. He wanted *her*.

Tonight that was what she needed more than absolutely everything.

Mila's eyes snapped open. It was far too dark to read anything in Seb's eyes, but that really didn't matter.

If anything, it helped. It reduced everything down to what she wanted and what he wanted. Which was to touch much more than just their hands.

Mila gripped his hand tighter and then, her gaze dropping to his lips, tugged, pulled him towards her.

Their lips met a split second before their bodies—chest to breast, hips to hips. Seb's hand dropped hers, only to appear near her waist, his other hand at her lower back, drawing her even closer.

Mila's hand curled up and behind his neck, her fingers combing into his hair.

Their mouths were momentarily as cool as the breeze, but as they kissed there was nothing but heat.

Seb showed no caution. He kissed her with the confidence of a man who knew what they both wanted—and he was right. All Mila wanted was to be closer, closer—luxuriating in the sensation of lips and teeth and tongue.

This was *all* want and *all* need. As wild as the ocean and as uncontrollable.

Mila slid her hand towards Seb's tie, tugging at it, and then at the top buttons of his shirt, frustrated that so much of him was covered in linen and silk. His skin felt impossibly hot beneath her fingertips, and then against her back, as Seb's hand searched for its own bare skin, finding it at her shoulder.

They barely broke apart for air, every kiss just fuelling the next. Their mouths and their bodies working together in search of that same goal of delicious sensation. Of heat and of need and of want.

But then it was over. As abruptly as it had begun and so suddenly that Mila reached for Seb automatically, her body refusing to accept the space now between them.

But the space was there, and her fingertips held nothing but thin air.

'We can't do this,' said Seb.

'Why not?'

It seemed the only possible question. There was nothing more right, right now, than that kiss. Mila was absolutely sure of that.

'This is wrong,' Seb said, and his unknowing contradiction was like a punch to her gut.

Reality descended.

'You've had a tough night. I shouldn't have done this.'

'*We* did this,' Mila said.

He shook his head. 'No. This is my mistake. This wasn't supposed to happen.'

'I didn't plan this either,' she said, but he wasn't really listening.

Instead he ran his hands through his hair, staring up at the sky.

As every second passed the *rightness* of what had just happened became less tangible.

'This can't happen,' Seb said, but Mila had the sense that he wasn't really speaking to her. 'It would change everything.'

He'd walked a few steps away, but now came

closer again, focusing again on Mila. Again the lack of light was frustrating. It was impossible to read whatever was in his eyes.

'I need you,' he said, rough and earnest. 'In my life. As my *friend. Not* like this. I won't risk our friendship. Not for a kiss. Not for anything.' A pause. 'I don't want this.'

A car drove past along the road above them, its lights briefly revealing Seb's gaze.

But Mila could see nothing. He'd retreated, shut up shop, boarded up his windows.

It took a few seconds for his words to start hurting. Maybe she'd already felt too much tonight. Surely soon she would run out of space.

But, no—the pain found a way. Alongside her father's rejection now lay Seb's. And beside that the faintest echo of Seb's very first rejection, all those years ago. When a teenage Mila's raw heart had first begun to build its armour.

Now she had fifteen years of further reinforcements, but tonight she'd let Blaine *and* Seb step right through.

That wouldn't happen again.

Mila retrieved her shoes and finally stepped around Seb, as she should have done what now felt a million hours ago.

She'd already ordered a taxi on her phone by the

time Seb joined her on the footpath a few minutes later.

He talked a bit, tried to get Mila to respond, but she just couldn't pay attention. Instead, with a frustration so intense it made her want to scream, she focused on doing everything in her power not to cry.

CHAPTER SEVEN

ON MONDAY, SEBASTIAN pushed open the door to Mila's shop with one shoulder, a takeaway coffee tray in his hand. Sheri was at the counter, looking every inch the university arts student that Seb knew her to be, complete with vintage eyeliner and purple Bettie Page-style hair.

She smiled as he approached her, and more broadly when he placed her coffee in front of her.

'Awesome,' she said. 'Thanks. Mila's out the back.'

Mila was carefully sliding a tray of pottery into the large kiln that hunkered against the side wall. She glanced at him, but for such a brief second that he had no chance to register if she was glad to see him or otherwise.

He suspected otherwise.

Her tone—if there *was* such a thing in text messages—had been terse over the weekend. She hadn't answered his calls.

'Mila—' he began, but she held up a hand.

'Give me a sec,' she said.

He waited as she swung the heavy door shut and then pushed a series of buttons on an electronic screen. The kiln beeped happily in response.

'Yes?' she asked, once she was done.

But she still didn't really look at him, instead walking over to the sink to wash her hands.

'I'm not happy with how things ended on Friday.'

Mila shrugged. 'That's a shame.' Her gaze zeroed in on the coffee tray. 'What do I owe you for the coffee?'

'*Nothing,*' he said. 'I'm not here just to bring you coffee.'

'Really?' she said. She turned, propping her butt against the sink cabinet. She wore skinny black jeans beneath a long artist's smock, liberally splashed with what he assumed was clay and glaze.

Her feet were clad only in flip flops, her toenails painted a vivid red. They drew his eye, and also drew an unwanted memory of bare feet on the beach, sinking into sand as he and Mila sank into each other.

'So what *do* you want, then?'

Mila's voice dragged him back to the present. Her tone was strong and direct—like the Mila he was used too. Not fractured or abandoned. He'd never seen Mila like she'd been on that beach, even as a teenager. Friday had been something else—a different level.

He'd hated to see Mila in pain. He'd hated to cause her pain.

'I want to fix this,' he said.

'I thought I'd made it clear how our relationship would progress from now on,' she said.

She was meeting his gaze now. Her big blue eyes were luminous.

'I don't want to just be another forgotten acquaintance on your friends list.'

'You want me to be a real friend?' Mila said, very calmly. 'Who you can have lunch with and buy coffee for—' she nodded at the cups he still held '—and chat about current events and our lives and stuff?'

He nodded, but he knew this wasn't headed anywhere good.

'But not to kiss on the beach under any circumstances, right? Just so we're both crystal-clear.'

He couldn't read her at all now. He didn't know what she meant.

'Did you want that to happen?' he asked, genuinely surprised. Although he wasn't sure if he was surprised by what she'd said or the fact that she'd said it.

He hadn't allowed himself to reflect on what had happened, and the tension between them well before that kiss. He'd only focused on the fact that it shouldn't have happened at all.

'No,' Mila said. 'I didn't.'

She said the words firmly, her gaze equally firm. But there was still something wrong. Something in the way she held herself and the way she looked at him. A vulnerability, perhaps, that made Seb want to fill the air with explanations.

'I just can't do this, Mila. And not just with you—this isn't about you. This is about *me*, and what a crappy husband I was, and how that proves I shouldn't do relationships, that I'm terrible at them. I'd just screw things up and hurt you like I hurt Steph. And I just can't face hurting you, and losing you, too—'

'It was a kiss, Seb, nothing more,' Mila said, again with that relentless calm. 'There's no need to talk about relationships.'

'Mila—'

She shook her head. 'You were right. It was a mistake.'

'So why—?'

'Can't we be friends?' she said. 'Because it's a waste of time. Just like it's a waste of time whenever I answer a call from my dad. Or am stupid enough to agree to see him. People make time for those who are important to them. Neither of us did that—for *years*. You know what? I can't be bothered with subterfuge.'

'I'm *not* like your father, Mila,' Seb said, his jaw tight.

'You're right,' Mila said simply. 'You have absolutely no reason to feel guilty for walking away.'

'I'm not walking away.'

Mila smiled sadly. 'You already did. So did I. Can't you see?'

It felt as if a hand was inside his chest, relentlessly smothering his heart. Until now Seb had refused to believe this could happen. This was fixable. It *had* to be. He *couldn't* lose Mila as well. He couldn't.

'For more than fifteen years we were almost inseparable. So what if we got busy and distracted and lazy—and if I've been a grieving, selfish ass? That doesn't erase our friendship. I don't believe you ever thought our friendship was over before Steph died. So why is it over now?'

He just didn't get it. He knew he'd stuffed up. He knew he'd hurt her. But he'd apologised. Even Mila had acknowledged the role that grief had played in his still unacceptable behaviour.

'Why do you want this so badly?' Mila asked.

She hadn't answered his question, but he was hardly in a position to push. Seb knew it would take only the slightest of nudges to lose her for ever.

It would be easy for him to repeat what he'd told her that first day—that he'd lost Steph and simply wanted Mila back in his life. But the way he felt right now: his throat tight, his shoulders thick with tension... It was more than that.

The idea of not seeing Mila again... It was causing him pain. Literal, physical pain.

'I need you, Mila.' His voice cracked. He hated that. *Hated* that.

He gave no further explanation. He didn't have one. He hated himself for delaying seeing Mila when he'd returned to Perth, for delaying his apology. But he'd been arrogant enough to believe that—beyond his own guilt—time wouldn't matter. That Mila would always be there. That they'd just step back into the easy friendship of the past.

He'd been wrong.

It hadn't happened. Their friendship was certainly no longer easy.

But that didn't change what he knew, unequivocally: he needed her.

Mila stepped closer, reaching towards the coffee tray he'd forgotten he was still holding. The tall cardboard cups leant precariously, but Mila plucked them to safety, then nodded somewhere behind him.

'You can chuck the tray in the recycling bin over there.'

He did so, obediently, unable to interpret Mila's expression. When he turned back Mila hadn't moved. But now she held out his coffee as she licked milk foam from her lips.

He took it and drank, but didn't taste the strong black liquid, still hot against his tongue. Every sense in his body was too busy waiting for Mila. He swallowed the coffee, but it didn't ease the suffocating tightness of his throat.

'Okay,' Mila said. 'Okay.'

They both stood in silence for a little while longer.

Eventually Mila smiled.

And finally Seb could breathe.

Later that week they played tennis again.

It had been Mila's idea, but she couldn't say she'd been looking forward to it.

Seb had arrived first. He was already out on court, but he was facing away from the car park when Mila's car pulled in, his phone pressed to his ear.

He wore similar attire to the last time they'd played and, like the last time they'd played, Mila was unable to do anything but admire his muscular form.

Mila also wore the same outfit as she had last time: a singlet, and tennis shorts that hit mid-thigh. For a moment at home she'd held a pair of old, long baggy shorts in her hands—before deciding she was being ridiculous. Her outfit was practical and sporty. Nothing more. And if they were to continue their friendship, then showing a bit of skin was *not* allowed to be an issue.

That was how Mila was approaching this. This situation with Seb. She would simply disallow any complications.

Mila and Seb were friends. Only. It was that simple.

It had to be.

Mila grabbed her tennis bag from her back seat before climbing out of her car and beginning her walk to the court.

On Monday, in the face of Seb's pain and unexpected desperation, it had suddenly become impossible for Mila to walk away from him. So that meant she needed to work out a plan. A plan to be there for Seb in his obvious time of need—and a way to move on from this unwanted, uncomfortable attraction.

On her own terms.

She hadn't answered Seb's question then—the reason why they simply couldn't continue their friendship. But that wasn't because the reason was unclear. The reasons, really.

Partly—there was guilt. There was still her loyalty to Stephanie, and the fact that even after all these years her promise to Steph still resonated somewhere inside her. But mainly the reason was that all that guilt wouldn't have mattered if Seb hadn't labelled their kiss as wrong, but had instead kissed her again, and again...

She wouldn't have cared. She would have thrown her promise to the wind and plummeted into wherever that kiss had taken them.

And that realisation was both galling and terrifying.

For her attraction to Seb was so intense—and so very, very, real—that she would have allowed herself to forget everything she'd learned. That her father had taught her—that her ex-fiancé had taught her. That even fourteen-year-old Seb had taught her.

Rejection hurt. Bone-deep.

How many times had she told herself not to put

herself in that situation again? *Every* time her father had let her down. The time when Ben had...

'Mila!'

Seb's smile was wide as he dropped his phone to his side. 'Sorry,' he said. 'Work call.'

Mila smiled back at him. It wasn't forced—being around Seb *did* make her smile. She just needed to ensure that it was always in a determinedly *friends only* type of way.

'How was your day?' Seb asked as Mila dropped her bag beside the net.

For the next few minutes they chatted casually—the latest on Seb's apartment block development, how quickly Mila's latest class had filled up. It was all very pleasant. As pleasant as their occasional texts over the past few days.

Seb hadn't dropped by with any more coffee. Maybe he'd guessed—rightly—that Mila needed some distance. But he'd stayed in touch, and been keen to catch up.

So here they were. Once again with the protection of the tennis net between them.

One set later Mila had started to relax. She'd won a tiebreaker—*convincingly*, she'd said. *Narrowly*, Seb had insisted, with a smile.

It was fun, she'd decided. Maybe this was what

their 'thing' could be. Weekly tennis. She could do that.

Later Seb had break point on Mila's serve. A deep ground stroke had sent Mila scrambling after the ball, and she'd managed only the weakest defensive lob in return. As the ball floated up and up Seb raced to the net, his racquet up and ready to hit a smash.

Just for a split second he glanced at Mila and winked—and that was just so one hundred per cent assured, cheeky Seb that Mila laughed out loud.

And then laughed even harder when his preemptive smugness led to his racquet hitting nothing but fresh air and the ball landing safely within the court—too far away, despite Seb's very best efforts to reach it.

He stood, bemused, hands on hips. 'I've got nothing,' he said, his eyes sparkling.

'Deuce,' Mila replied happily, then went on to win the game.

They laughed again when Mila feigned a racquet-throwing tantrum after a silly double fault, and Seb laughed at Mila's whoop of victory when a lucky net cord fell her way.

Mila won in straight sets, and they both jogged to the net to shake hands—an old habit that Mila didn't think twice about.

Until, that was, Seb actually held her hand in his. Warm, big, strong.

And just like that all the camaraderie, all the *friendship* of the past ninety minutes, evaporated. All that remained was the reality that for the first time since they'd kissed amongst the sand dunes they were touching. Skin to skin.

Electricity shot up Mila's arm, so shocking that for a moment, her brain went blank.

She couldn't remember any of the reasons why they were only friends. She couldn't remember why leaping over the net and into his arms would be a truly terrible idea.

But then Seb let go.

'You're very fit,' he said quickly. Randomly.

'Pardon me?' she said, although she'd heard him. She needed a moment to locate her thoughts.

He'd taken a step back and rubbed his hand down his thigh, as if wiping away Mila's touch. Irrationally, that stung.

'You barely raised a sweat,' he said, trying again.

That wasn't even close to true. 'I'm a sporadic gym-user,' Mila said, keen for pointless conversation to ease the sudden tension between them. 'I got into it a bit when I was with Ben. Now I go when I remember. Or just go for walks with Ivy and Nate. Mostly that, actually.'

Perfect—another man, her sister and a baby were the perfect topics to divert attention.

'What happened with Ben?' Seb asked.

Mila had been looking into the darkness beyond Seb's shoulder and the court fencing, but now she forced herself to meet his gaze.

Maybe Seb was grasping at the opportunity to talk about absolutely anything. Or more likely he felt nothing when they touched and was simply having a perfectly reasonable conversation.

'He cheated on me,' Mila said baldly. There was really no other way to say it.

'Oh, Mila—' Seb began.

But Mila wasn't about to let him continue. She didn't need to see the pity in his gaze as he realised that—yes—yet another man had *not* chosen Mila.

'It's old news, Seb, I'd rather not talk about it.'

She grabbed her water bottle from beside her bag and took a long, long drink. She made sure she was smiling by the time she packed her racquet back in its bag and as they walked together back to their cars. Their conversation moved on to the trivial, and by the time Mila was in her car and driving home she'd just about convinced herself that she'd imagined her reaction to Seb's touch.

And besides—it didn't really matter, did it? They were just friends.

* * *

It was the perfect summer evening—warm, but with a sea breeze cooling their skin. The Fremantle beach was dotted with open-sided tents and food trucks, and a busker sang beneath a zig-zag of festoon lights—although the sun was still yet to complete its descent. Beneath the purple and red sky children ran and laughed, and their parents held cardboard trays piled high with food. Tourists took photos with bulky cameras and teenagers took phone selfies against the backdrop of surf and sand and towering Norfolk pines.

'Cool, huh?' Mila smiled up at Seb, her lovely eyes covered by her oversized sunglasses.

Seb nodded his agreement. He'd invited her for a drink after work, but Mila had suggested the beach markets instead. It was a good idea—more casual, more people.

Although that had been why Seb had suggested a drink in the first place: because it *shouldn't* matter if he and Mila had a drink in a bar—it shouldn't feel like anything but two friends catching up after work. It shouldn't feel private, or intimate, or date-like.

But it seemed that maybe Mila had thought it would. Maybe Seb did, too. It didn't really matter—the important thing was that he and Mila were hanging out together, just as he'd wanted. As friends.

Over the past couple of weeks, since the film premiere, it had become clear that they were both on the same page, that they wanted to remain within firm 'friends only' boundaries. There'd been a few blips—that first, post-kiss tennis game, for example.

He'd been quite pleased at how well that match had gone, despite the distraction of Mila, and her obvious gorgeousness in her tennis gear, and her legs that went on for ever. He'd just about convinced himself that he was back to being objective Seb, capable of simply admiring the attractiveness of his *friend* without it meaning anything more, and then they'd shaken hands...

How stupid that such a G-rated touch had robbed him of his ability to think. For long moments, Seb hadn't been able to grasp at even one reason why he and Mila couldn't be much, much more than friends.

Fortunately he'd come to his senses, and Mila had seemed utterly unaware. But Seb had made sure there'd been no handshake at the end of their match the following week, though—just to be safe.

And now here they were, on a postcard-perfect beach, surrounded by the scents of falafel and satay and pizza. Mila was a few steps ahead, scouting out their dinner options. It was exactly what he wanted—the easy, comfortable, reliable friendship of his past.

Because he'd realised, when faced with losing Mila, that she was the only constant in his now topsy-turvy life. Everything had changed, Everything was no longer how it was meant to be. His friendships—in London and at Fyfe Technology—had drifted, and floated away, not strong enough to sustain his international relocation. He didn't mind—he'd eventually make new friends, find new mates to go cycling with, to invite over for a beer. But he wasn't ready for that yet. He wasn't ready to share his history with just anyone, or to invite others into this new and uncertain phase of his life.

Mila already knew him. Not the details of the past few years—and certainly not the mess of his marriage—but she did know *him*. He didn't have to explain himself to her. He didn't have to be anyone else for her. He just got to *be* with her.

Except when he was derailed by this continued, unwanted attraction.

But he could handle it. Surely it would pass with time.

Mila pointed at a tent to their right, then looked

back at Seb over her shoulder. She wore a pale blue summer dress, her shoulders golden in the setting sun.

'Oh, *look*—crêpes!'

They ended up completing a full lap of all the food options before spotting a park bench, shaded by the outstretched boughs of a Norfolk pine, which they promptly claimed. In order to sample most of the food up for offer, they'd agreed to share—with one of them heading out for food while the other saved the seat.

Seb set out, returning with a shredded beef burger, topped with a shiny brioche bun. Mila finished her half first, and headed back out into the crowd for their second course.

The sun continued its gradual fall into the ocean, where two container ships interrupted the perfect line of the horizon. As Seb sat there, wiping barbecue sauce from his fingers with a napkin, he felt for the first time as if...

'Is this seat taken?'

Seb looked up at the sound of a soft, very female voice. The woman was short, blonde, and very pretty, with long tumbling hair and warm brown eyes.

Unthinkingly, he ran his thumb over the place

where his wedding band had once been—but of course it wasn't there.

'Oh,' he said, wondering if he was jumping to conclusions. Maybe she genuinely just needed somewhere to sit?

'Seb?'

It was Mila, cradling a neatly closed white cardboard box and a tray with two forks stabbed into a mound of paella.

'Oh!' the blonde woman said. 'I'm so sorry. I thought—' She was blushing, her gaze darting to her feet. 'Have a lovely day!'

Then she was gone.

'Who was that?' Mila asked, settling onto the bench. She put the box down beside her—away from Seb. 'Dessert,' she said with a grin. 'It's a surprise.'

Then she carefully served out the paella into the second tray that had been hiding beneath the first.

'I have no idea,' Seb said, and then had his first mouthful of paella—all spicy and delicious.

'So she was hitting on you?'

Seb coughed, a piece of rice stuck in his throat. 'I guess,' he said, really not wanting to have this conversation with Mila.

'She was pretty. Do you want to go talk to her? I won't mind.'

'What?'

Mila shrugged, waving a piece of chorizo on the end of her fork. 'Go on. Don't let me stop you.'

She was still wearing her sunglasses, so it was impossible to read her expression.

'Don't you remember what I said? About how I'm terrible at relationships?'

'That was just to make me feel—' But she didn't finish the sentence, instead taking off her sunglasses and meeting his gaze. '*That* wasn't a relationship. That was a woman angling to ask you out. You could do that.'

'No,' he said, unequivocally. 'I could not.'

'Why not?'

Mila was focused on her paella now, chasing pieces of meat and vegetables about in the rice. She sounded completely relaxed.

Seb had lost his appetite.

'I wasn't a very good husband, Mila. I don't want to put someone else through that again.'

'That doesn't mean you can't date again. Have some fun.'

He honestly hadn't really thought about it. In London, his one-night stands had left him empty. And now, back in Perth, there was Mila...

No. He simply wasn't ready.

He said so.

'I get that,' Mila said. 'That's understandable. I just wanted to make sure your decision wasn't anything to do with me.'

She met his gaze now, absolutely direct. It was almost as if she was daring him to agree. Or disagree. Seb had no idea.

'It isn't,' Seb said.

'Good,' she said, looking out to the ocean. 'You know, I kind of get it… After what happened with Ben I didn't think I ever wanted to do that again.' A pause. '*Ever.*' She finished her paella. 'But, you know, that is pretty unrealistic. I've been to both my sisters' weddings over the past couple of years. I know I want that too. To be in love like that. To be loved like that. I think the trick will be to work out a way to protect myself.'

'From what?' he said.

'You know…' she said, with half a smile. 'The messy bits that hurt. Like your ex-fiancé hooking up with a girl from work. They're engaged now.'

'Ouch,' Seb said.

'Yup.' A grin. 'But that's okay. I think I fought too long for that relationship to work. The signs were there. Kind of like my dad, in a way. I let hope drive my delusions…illusions…whatever. I won't do *that* again.'

'So how will you do it? How will you protect yourself?'

Mila shook her head. 'I'm working on it,' she said.

They were both quiet for a while. Two little girls with fairies painted on their cheeks came running past them, squealing and waving sequined wands.

'Can you hurry up and finish your dinner, Seb?' Mila said suddenly—and brightly. 'Because we *have* to try these cupcakes. One is triple choc *and* salted caramel. How is that even *possible*?'

CHAPTER EIGHT

SEB WAS ON the phone when Mila walked into his shop on Tuesday.

He stood at the back, a shoulder propped against the bare brick wall. The new first floor was in, although the rafters were still exposed. Mila could hear the activity of tradesmen upstairs: the murmur of conversation punctuated by the occasional whir of a drill.

Aaron, one of the labourers, was sweeping up a pile of rubble and sawdust near the shop window. He smiled a greeting. He was young and tall, with his red-blond hair arranged in a man bun and a cheeky glint to his eye.

They'd spoken once before, when Mila had asked if she could retrieve some old coloured glass bottles from the skip. She'd thought maybe she could use the glass in some of her pieces. Or just use them as skinny vases. She wasn't sure—she just thought they were pretty.

Mila found herself smoothing her T-shirt against

her hips as she walked towards Seb, but she stopped herself. She didn't have to worry about looking nice for Seb. Besides, she was wearing a variation of what she wore every day—skinny jeans and a loose T-shirt with a loud print. Today the print was of nasturtiums. She wasn't trying to impress *anyone*. Certainly not Seb.

He'd seen her as soon as she'd walked in, his smile wide and welcoming. Mila grinned back. *See. This was nice.*

She'd popped over to see if he was free for lunch. She'd made too much pasta last night, so thought she'd invite him up to her place for leftovers. Surely you couldn't get more relaxed and friend-like than *that*.

Although with the way her heart accelerated as she took in his work shirt, shorts and heavy boots…which she still wasn't used to and still really rather liked…she decided that maybe she'd bring their bowls of penne downstairs, and they could eat in the workshop—with Sheri as a chaperon, of sorts.

Oh, God. She was being ridiculous. Because what had happened on Friday at the beach markets had been a *good* thing. She was at pains to remind herself of that. Was there any better way to define their friendship then to bring another women into the equation? Seb should have gone after her, and spoken to her. She'd looked nice. Very pretty, too.

There was simply no reason why he shouldn't have. Least of all because of the way Mila had felt when she'd spotted them, her arms full with paella and a box of cupcakes.

She should probably have expected that seeing Seb with another woman would feel like a knife to her heart. That seemed dramatic now, but it was how she'd felt. She'd stood there for a moment, utterly still, her insides all sliced up with pain.

Which was silly. She had no right.

Seb had made it clear—for him, being with Mila was wrong, even though for her it had felt right. And she just couldn't argue with that. He could wrap it up in talk of being *'terrible at relationships'*, blah-blah-blah. But how stupid—as if Seb would never be with anyone else after Steph.

He just didn't want to be with *her*.

Seb asked the person on the phone to hold on for a moment, before holding his phone against his chest. 'Sorry, Mila, I'll only be another minute. I'm having a major issue with this supplier—'

'That's fine,' she said with another smile. She wasn't in a hurry.

'How are you, Mila?' Aaron asked, behind her.

Glad for something to do, she turned to face

him. He really was quite handsome, although in a surfer, music festival kind of way.

'I'm good,' she said. 'Busy day?'

They chatted for a few minutes. Aaron had recently bought a new car that he described enthusiastically. Cars weren't really Mila's thing, but then she'd told all and sundry when she'd first got her new kiln, so she understood the excitement of a big, shiny toy.

From the corner of her eye Mila saw Seb turn slightly away from them. His words were still calm, but there was definitely a layer of steel in what he said.

'So I was wondering…would you like to go see it? With me?'

'Pardon me?' Mila said, suddenly realising the conversation had moved on from cars and their stereo systems.

Aaron's gaze was confident and his lips quirked upwards. 'I asked if you wanted to see *Agent X*— you know, that spy movie? It's cheap night tonight.' He paused. 'Not that I'd mind paying for full-priced tickets for you, of course.'

Mila laughed at his aplomb, then realised he was being serious.

'Oh,' she said.

'Unless,' Aaron said, 'you've got something

going with my boss? Only I heard him tell one of the other guys you were just friends, so I thought—'

Ouch.

But it was true—once again, she really had nothing to be upset about.

'No,' she said. 'We *are* just friends.'

Aaron grinned.

Mila was flattered, and Aaron did seem very nice—if young—but...

'Thanks for the invite, but—'

Seb had finished his call and turned back to face them. She couldn't read his expression—not at all. He was just watching them. Waiting for Mila to finish her conversation.

What had she expected? Jealousy?

'Actually,' Mila said, 'that sounds great. What time?'

They swapped phone numbers before Aaron went back to his work and Mila walked over to Seb.

'Hot date?' he asked with a grin.

Maybe his smile was forced. *Maybe* he didn't meet her gaze. Or maybe he was simply pleased for her.

It didn't matter.

'Something like that,' she said, with a deliberately broad smile. 'So, do you feel like some penne marinara? I made it and, without a word of a lie, it's awesome.'

Seb went for a really long walk after dinner. His apartment was in East Perth, so he went past the cricket ground and down to the Swan River. He shared the path with late-night dog walkers, joggers and cyclists—the latter's headlights blinding in the darkness.

He hadn't bothered to dress appropriately, so he was still wearing what he'd changed into after work—jeans, flip flops, a faded old T-shirt. So he didn't really fit in with all the Lycra and the neon running shoes—but then, he wasn't here to exercise. Although his pace wasn't completely sedate. He found himself walking faster and faster, his shoes slapping on the bitumen in an attempt to outpace his thoughts.

Maybe.

Until now it had been easy to fill his brain and his day with stuff that didn't involve Mila. With work, mostly. A new site purchase, an investor meeting, a marketing consultant. Then, later, with food. He must have perused every possible home delivery option, and then spent way too long reading online reviews before finally ordering. When his food had eventually arrived he hadn't been hungry. Instead he'd just pushed it around with a fork before eventually conceding defeat and constructing a little tower of plastic containers in his fridge.

So now he'd run out of things to distract his brain with. All that was left was Mila. Mila on her date. With Aaron.

He thought he'd handled things quite well in his shop. He'd teased her, as was appropriate given he was her *friend*. And Aaron seemed to be a good guy. He was hard-working, reliable and enthusiastic about his job—all reasons why Seb should like him. Until today he had. Tonight…he didn't.

He didn't like him at all.

He'd tried telling himself that he was worried about Mila. That after Ben cheating on her, and her father letting her down—after losing Steph— the last thing she needed was to be hurt again.

After all, that was why he'd ended their kiss. Why he'd realised it was wrong. He just couldn't be responsible for Mila being hurt again. He would not allow it.

But that wasn't the only reason he didn't like Mila's date. This wasn't brotherly-type concern.

Far from it.

Maybe Mila was okay with him talking to other women—as she'd said at the markets. With him having relationships with other women.

As they'd talked that night he'd agreed with everything she'd said: in theory.

Because it was one thing for them both to talk about their hypothetical relationships in a hypothetical future. It was another for the future to be here right now.

And right this instant Mila was on a date with another man. A man who wasn't him.

He *hated* that.

The sea breeze was cool against Seb's skin. He headed towards the new Elizabeth Quay and the bell tower, where restaurants perched along the water. Even on a Tuesday night people bustled about—it was a perfect early summer evening, before the weather became too hot to do anything but swim.

Seb slowed his pace to a dawdle, and then came to a complete stop just to the side of the footpath. He stood on the grass, watching the small white caps on the river's tiny waves.

He wanted Mila.

But he couldn't have her.

He couldn't risk hurting her and losing her.

Because she was all he had left.

He couldn't face the idea of his world without Mila.

On the beach, she'd been so very wrong to label herself a substitute for Steph. That was doing a disservice to both women. Steph had irreplaceably been Steph, while Mila was irreplaceably Mila.

He'd never imagined a world without either of them—even as he'd known his marriage was failing and that his relationship with Steph had become irreparable.

For Steph to be gone was still impossible—she'd been so full of life, so full of dreams. She'd deserved a future no longer married to him. She'd deserved a future, full stop.

But Mila was still here. She was real, alive, and still part of his world. He was not going to ruin that. He *would* not.

A splash in the inky black river drew Seb's attention. But the river was calm. Then again—a subtle splash, this time in Seb's line of vision, a shift in the shadows beneath the moonlight.

A dolphin. Two. Swimming together, their fins appearing and disappearing amongst the waves, a pair perfectly in sync.

His phone vibrated in his back pocket, and by the time he'd retrieved it the dolphins were gone.

A text message—from Mila.

I need to see you.

CHAPTER NINE

BY THE TIME Seb had walked back to his apartment block Mila was already there. She was waiting in the foyer, pacing a short path in front of the mirrored lifts.

She paused the instant Seb stepped through the automatic doors, making as if to hurry towards him—but then she stopped. Instead she waited for him to approach her.

'Nice place,' Mila said, meeting his gaze.

He shrugged. 'It's fine,' he said. 'I plan to build something like this—but better—some day soon.'

She nodded sharply. 'You will.'

She'd wrapped her arms around herself even though it was perfectly temperature-controlled in here—not too hot, not too cold. She wore skinny blue jeans and spiky heels. Her jacket was of some type of faded grey linen, with sections of a silky pink camisole top visible where her arms weren't gripping herself tightly. She looked fantastic.

He wasn't being objective.

'Can I come up?' she asked.

There was no point acknowledging that it was a bad idea—to himself or to Mila. 'Sure,' he said.

He reached past her to push the elevator's 'up' button, then when the doors opened gestured for Mila to walk into the small space before him. Her heels clattered loudly on the marble floor as she fidgeted inside the elevator—walking over to the back to run a finger along the railing, then over to the side, and then simply standing almost exactly in the middle, shifting her weight from foot to foot.

Seb scanned his access key and pressed the button for his floor. He didn't move as the doors swished shut, not sure what to do. Keeping his distance from Mila seemed the best idea. He didn't know why she was here.

'Not the penthouse?' Mila asked as they stepped onto his floor.

'No,' he said with a shrug. 'New business. New priorities.'

Not that he was exactly slumming it. He still had half of the entire floor to himself. Unlocking his front door revealed a tastefully decorated, luxury serviced apartment—and, more importantly, the view across the river he'd just walked beside to the twinkling lights of the South Perth foreshore.

'Nice,' Mila said simply, walking before him into the main living space.

It was an open-plan conglomeration of gourmet kitchen, dining room and living room, looking out over a wide herringbone-paved balcony complete with a barbecue he never used and an outdoor setting he used nearly every day. He was definitely taking advantage of the Perth sun after years in far less sunny London.

'Can we go outside?' Mila said. 'It's a bit stuffy in here.'

It wasn't, but he followed her onto the balcony. Since she'd greeted him she hadn't met his gaze at all. He didn't think he'd ever seen her so highly strung. She was constantly moving—crossing and uncrossing her arms, lacing her fingers together, touching every different texture she found: the grain of the jarrah outdoor table, the shine of the stainless steel barbecue lid, the rough surface of the stone-hewn abstract sculpture in one corner.

'This is really ugly,' she said.

It was, but that wasn't the point. 'What's going on, Mila?' Seb asked. 'Why do you need to see me?'

Finally she turned to look at him—to *really* look at him. He stood in front of the still open sliding door. Mila was metres away from him, near the balcony railing.

'Aaron kissed me,' she said.

Seb simply had no words.

Mila filled up the silence. 'He's a really nice guy, it turns out. And he's tall. And hot. In a really, really young kind of way...'

'Am I supposed to offer you congratulations?'

'No,' Mila said. '*No.* That's the point. I wanted to kiss him. I think so, anyway. Or maybe I just wanted to *want* to kiss him. I don't know.' She pivoted on her heel to face out towards the river. 'But kissing him wasn't great. Wasn't even good. It was awful, actually. And awfully quick. It was over in seconds—I just couldn't do it. I knew it was wrong. Really wrong.'

Seb walked up to stand beside her, also leaning against the rail.

Mila ran her hands through her hair, her fingers leaving it all haphazard. 'It was wrong, totally wrong, because...'

And now her avalanche of words ended.

She turned again, propping her hip against the rail so she faced Seb. He did the same, although their casual poses were failing in any attempt to relax the growing tension between them.

Mila met his gaze and held it. He could practically see it—that one last boulder, teetering at the top, waiting for Mila to open her mouth again.

'Why was it wrong, Mila?'

She glared at him. 'You *know*. You do—and don't pretend you don't.'

But he really wanted to pretend. Everything would be simpler if he did.

Yet they both just stood there.

'It was wrong because of you,' Mila said eventually, unnecessarily. 'It was wrong because of this. Because of us.'

She gestured between them, pointing to Seb and then to herself.

'I hate this,' Mila said, very softly.

'Why did you come here?' Seb asked.

'Because I was angry. At myself. At you.'

'Why are you angry?'

'Because this shouldn't be happening.'

'I know,' he said. But he needed to know her reasons. 'Why not?'

'Because it isn't how it's supposed to be. I'm not supposed to feel this way about you. You're *Seb*—you're Steph's husband. You're my best friend's husband.'

'Not any more.'

'I know,' she said. She ran a hand through her hair, looking past him towards that ugly sculpture. 'And that isn't even really the reason. I just don't want to feel this way. Because I know what will happen. I know—' She stopped abruptly, then looked straight at him. 'And I'm angry at *you*. For not walking away when I told you to. I needed you to walk away, Seb...'

'I could never walk away from you, Mila.'

She looked up at the sky, rolling her eyes.

He didn't understand—how could she not believe him? 'Why did you need to see me, Mila?' he asked again, this time with a hard edge. 'What did you want to happen?'

He couldn't work it out—what she was thinking, what she wanted. But he did understand the tension between them.

'I don't know,' she said, but Seb didn't really believe her.

She shouldn't have come. And he definitely shouldn't be glad she was here. But she had, and he was.

'What do *you* want to happen?' she asked.

'I don't know,' he said, lying too.

There wasn't much space between them. A metre...maybe a little less.

Mila still held his gaze. He wished hers was unreadable, but it wasn't—not any more. He was sure his wasn't either.

All he had to do was reach for her...

And that would be it.

It would change everything. Their friendship—the friendship that was so important to him, that he needed so badly—would be altered for ever.

And Mila... Was this really what she wanted?

'I just want tonight,' Mila whispered, reading his mind.

And with that he was losing himself in those eyes, falling into their depths. He needed to touch her. He needed Mila. There was no going back.

He shifted his weight, pushing himself away from the railing. Mila remained still, but watched him. He stepped closer, with plans to drag her into his arms. But then he paused.

Instead he leant forward, bending closer, until her breath was against his lips. Her breath hitched.

Heat flooded Seb's body. He wasn't even touching her, yet every cell in his body was on high alert, desperate for Mila.

Then, finally, he kissed her. It just seemed fitting for their lips to meet first, for their kiss to be their focus—maybe to give Mila that one last chance to back away from the point of no return.

Because Seb knew he didn't have the strength to do it himself.

Her lips were plump, soft. Their kiss was intimate. Different from that kiss on the beach. More considered, more knowing. This was a kiss without a question—this was a kiss with a destination.

And Mila was definitely coming along for the ride.

Mila's hands were suddenly behind his neck; his were at her waist. And then she was in his arms, pressed as close as she could be.

Their kiss deepened as Seb's hand slid beneath Mila's camisole top, finding warm, smooth skin at her back. Mila slid her hands downwards, greedily discovering the shape of his shoulders and his chest.

His lips moved from her mouth to her jaw, to her neck—desperate to explore all of her, to taste all of her.

Mila continued her own exploration, her hands shoving up his T-shirt, feeling his skin hot beneath her touch.

Somehow they were back inside. Seb was backing her against the nearest wall. Mila was smiling and sighing against his mouth as they kissed.

But even now—even as his whole world was focused on Mila and how she felt, how *this* felt— Seb knew what he was doing. Knew what he was risking.

But he couldn't make himself stop. He couldn't

walk away from this—this maelstrom of need and desire. He needed this. Needed her. Needed tonight.

It would have to be enough.

When Mila woke it was still dark.

She rolled over in Seb's bed, hoping for an alarm clock or something that would tell her the time, but there was none.

Her phone was in her bag, abandoned somewhere in Seb's cavernous living area, so that couldn't help her.

Not that the time really mattered. What would she do with the information, anyway? Work out if it was an acceptable time to call a taxi and make a run for it back to her place? Or maybe, if it was still truly the middle of the night, use the time as an excuse to simply close her eyes again and snuggle closer to Seb's gorgeous warmth?

She didn't really need to know the time to do either of those things. Mila knew that. Either were viable options, regardless of the time.

One was the better option, of course. She should go. But instead she stayed exactly where she was. Naked, but not quite touching Seb, a thin expensive-feeling sheet covering them both.

Her eyes had adjusted to the darkness. It was a nice

room, although understandably devoid of any personality. The large bed had a stitched fabric buttoned headboard, and the bedside tables were spindly and clutter-free. Where Mila lay, she faced the door to the hallway. A large abstract canvas decorated the wall immediately opposite her, aligned with the door. It was too dark to work out the colours—they were simply dark splashes and swirls against a pale background. Mila had been too wrapped up in Seb to notice it when the lights had still been on.

She smiled at the memory.

Maybe she didn't need to know the time. Without it the night remained unanchored to reality. Like a dream. Perfect, with no regrets.

Seb shifted behind her, breathing with the steady, deep pattern of sleep.

Mila rolled over so she faced Seb again. He was also on his side, but it was impossible to make out any details in the darkness. She could watch his shoulders lift with his breathing, the shape of his body silhouetted against the window in the almost blackness…

'Mila…' he said, after a while.

'Sebastian.'

She never said his full name. Tonight, the longer word sounded like an endearment.

He reached out, drawing a finger along her jaw. 'You are so beautiful,' he said, very softly.

His thumb brushed against her bottom lip, and she couldn't have spoken if she'd wanted to. She realised she'd been restraining herself from touching Seb. Whatever reason she'd had for doing that instantly evaporated and became impossible to justify. Why, oh, why would she want to do anything *but* touch Sebastian Fyfe?

And so she did—exploring his face the way he'd explored hers, delicately tracing his eyebrows, his cheekbones, his nose, his lips.

She was rediscovering a face she'd known almost her whole life. But it was not the face of a boy any longer. Tonight it was almost unfamiliar—foreign to her. But then, that made sense, didn't it? Yesterday Seb had been a lifelong friend. Tonight he was her lover.

Mila waited for regret to descend.

But it didn't.

It would.

But right now that didn't matter. Right now it was dark. Right now time stood still.

Mila leant closer and kissed him.

She was having a shower. Seb was awake, sitting up in bed, reading some emails on his phone. From the shower Mila could see him through the open en-suite bathroom door, the shape of one propped knee tenting the sheet, his bare chest golden in the lamplight. He could probably turn the light off now, though. It was morning.

Mila turned her face upwards, directly into the spray of water, her eyes tight shut. This was all very domestic. Not quite comfortable, but not entirely awkward either.

She hadn't left as she'd intended, in yesterday's clothes under the cover of darkness. He hadn't asked her to, either. Although maybe he was just being polite.

She didn't know what the rules were in this situation. How did you have a one-night stand with a friend? Or someone who had once been a friend? Mila didn't know how to define Seb in her life any more. The definition had changed too much recently. A few weeks ago she'd thought she'd never see him again. Then suddenly he was a daily presence in her life, and recently there'd been glimpses of the friendship they'd once had. But now—now she didn't know what to call Seb.

Ex-something, though. Ex-friend…ex-lover. Because this was it, of course. After last night and this morning they were done.

She'd known it last night—known exactly what

she was doing when she'd come to Seb's apartment. She'd just focused on her need to see him—on her need *for* him—and allowed herself to do so: just for one night.

Seb had asked her at the beach markets how she would protect herself. Well, when it came to Seb and her decision to see him last night her plan had been simple.

It would only be one night.

I just want tonight.

One night she could handle. One night would not create expectations of a future and those delusions she was so apt to create.

And so she was safe, within her self-determined, one-night-only time box. Ivy had told her about time boxes, although she suspected they were rather different for mining project management. And in her time box Mila had been able to kiss Seb again, to discover his body, to sleep with him. Despite all the reasons why she shouldn't.

And it had been amazing. Incredible. Better than she could have imagined. So good that she couldn't regret it. She just couldn't.

But now that it was morning, and she had reached the end of her time box, reality was starting to descend even if regret did not. And the most obvious reality—the most important—was that she'd just slept with her best friend's husband.

Oh, she knew that wasn't strictly true any longer. She even knew that Steph would be the last person to expect Mila to stand by a teenage promise from beyond the grave. And, truth be told, Mila didn't *truly* feel guilty, as such.

But she did feel intensely aware, right now, of Steph. Suddenly Steph's loss felt raw. Raw in a way it hadn't for many months.

Mila turned beneath the water, bowing her head forward as her throat tightened. Water gushed over her hair, pushing it forward and into her eyes, but she didn't care. Silent tears mingled amongst the spray.

Seb's feet came into her watery view, just outside the shower. She lifted her gaze, then ran her fingers through her hair, pushing it back from her forehead.

'You okay?' he asked.

He'd been about to join her—his nakedness made that obvious. The last time Mila had seen Seb completely naked—in the daylight—would be twenty or more years ago. Amongst twirling sprinkler heads and shrieks of laughter.

Now he looked utterly different. And not the way she'd expected Seb to grow up. This Seb had all the extra muscles of a man with a physical job, not the lanky geekiness of the adult Seb she remembered. His shoulders were broad, his pectorals and stomach muscles defined, his legs powerful.

He was gorgeous—that was a fact. Strong. The tradesman's tan—where his olive skin abruptly became paler in the shape of a T-shirt and work shorts—did not even slightly distract from his perfection.

'Mila?'

She shook her head.

'You're not okay?' he asked. He stepped closer, as if to join her—or to check on her. Who knew?

'No, no,' she said firmly. 'I'm fine. Just getting out, though. It's all yours.'

He blinked, clearly confused.

Mila stepped aside, leaving the water running so he could step immediately beneath its warmth. She kept her distance, knowing that if she touched him she wouldn't be leaving the shower.

She felt his eyes on her as she grabbed a fluffy white towel and dried herself. For the first time she was aware of *her* nakedness. Was he reflecting, as well, on how her body had changed now that she was all grown-up? Or was he thinking of the other girl who'd run shrieking through those sprinklers all those years ago? Whose grown-up body he'd been far more familiar with. That he would've known almost as well as his own.

Suddenly it was all too much.

Her grief. Steph. Her time box. Seb.

Her procrastination was definitely over. She needed to leave. Not to be there any more.

I need to go.

So she did.

In his kitchen, she scrawled a note on the back of a takeaway menu. Seb hadn't noticed her retreat. Or maybe he was just more *au fait* with how one should behave the morning after.

It didn't matter—what he thought, what we would have said if she'd given him the chance to say goodbye.

Why would it? She'd been crystal-clear: *I just want tonight.*

And the night was over.

CHAPTER TEN

EACH WEEK SEB caught up with his parents for dinner.

Usually it was at a nice restaurant—his mum was a bit of a foodie, and took a lot of joy in sharing her favourite meals with her 'favourite child'. He was also her *only* child, although that didn't really lessen the sentiment. In the months he'd been back in Perth he'd yet to eat dinner at his parents' place. He'd barely visited, actually. Deliberately. And this hadn't gone unnoticed by his always shrewd parents.

They never said anything—they were good like that—but his mum would invite him over occasionally. Never with any pressure, never with any questions as to why he consistently declined—but she'd still ask him. As if prodding a bruise: *Does this still hurt too much, darling?*

As luck would have it, this week his mum, Monique, had invited him over for Sunday dinner.

And she hadn't been at all successful in hiding her surprise when he'd accepted.

Seb parked his car in front of the four-car garage located just to the side of his parents' mammoth home. It had been his mum and dad's dream home when it had been built—Seb still remembered the excitement of the day they'd moved in, when his parents had run around exploring the rooms as excited as the pre-school-age Seb had been.

Over the years the house had been modernised, its exterior rendered to hide all that once fashionable feature brick, and Seb's old bedroom converted to a guest room many moons ago. But it would always feel like home to Seb—the place intrinsically linked with so many of his childhood memories.

He'd had the best pool in the street, for example—complete with a slide and a small diving board—which had just been *the coolest thing ever*. It had been a hub for his friends—and the backdrop to many of Mila, Steph and Seb's adventures.

They'd played Marco Polo, they'd hosted pool parties, and they'd even shared a bottle of peach schnapps in the small pool house, aged fifteen and sixteen. That hadn't ended well—with sore heads and furious parents.

But it was his memories with Steph—just Steph—that made it so hard for Seb to visit this place.

Laughing together in his bedroom as they'd studied—with parent-prescribed door open, of course. Steph joining his family for dinner, charming his parents. That one night after Steph's Year Twelve ball in the pool house...

Seb climbed out of his car, slamming the door harder than he'd intended. It was dusk, and huge jacaranda trees were throwing long shadows across the Fyfe mansion. Twin jacarandas also stood outside the mansion to the left: the mansion that had once belonged to Steph's parents. Not any more, though. They'd sold up shortly after the funeral. Now a millionaire mobile app entrepreneur lived there, his mum had said. Complete with the sunshine-yellow Lamborghini parked in the drive.

While he understood why her parents had moved, it didn't seem possible that it was no longer 'Steph's place'. He'd always thought of it that way, even when they'd been living together in London.

He'd loved Steph. Really loved her. Once they'd been inseparable: that annoyingly happy couple that never argued. But as things had begun to fracture in their relationship Seb had wondered if maybe they'd married too young. They'd grown up together—but maybe they'd still had some grow-

ing up to do after they'd become husband and wife.
Maybe if they hadn't both got caught up in their
London dreams—if marriage hadn't conveniently
provided Seb with the visa that Steph had by de-
fault through her mum's British heritage...

Maybe, maybe, maybe. Maybe they shouldn't
have got married.

No.

Seb couldn't wish away his marriage. He couldn't
regret what they'd had. Once it had been special.

But he *could* regret his single-minded refusal to
address the cracks—and later canyons—that had
appeared between them.

He'd failed Stephanie. Driven her away, and
driven her to—

'Honey?'

His mother stood at the top of the limestone steps
before the grand front door, a short distance away.
Seb realised he hadn't moved, had simply been
standing beside his car, staring blankly out at the
street he'd grown up on.

'Mum!' he said with a big smile, striding towards her.

She watched him carefully, not bothering to con-
ceal her 'worried parent' expression.

'I'm okay,' Seb said, pre-empting her question
as he sprang up the oversized steps. 'Really.'

He followed his mum indoors. She talked about dinner as she led him down the hallway: she'd cooked something new, with salmon and something fancy that possibly sounded French.

His dad was in the kitchen, his hip propped against the large granite-topped island, a beer in his hand. The huge space faced a dining and living area of similar scale, and beyond that were large picture windows overlooking the glass-fenced pool and a spacious grassed area beyond.

'You finally made it,' his dad said.

'*Kevin,*' his mum said. 'Don't be so insensitive.'

He shrugged. 'It's an observation—nothing more.'

Seb nodded. Once he would have been equally matter-of-fact. He'd learnt a lot about life's shades of grey in the past eighteen months.

'I thought there might be too many memories here,' he said. He might as well be matter-of-fact about that too.

'Are there?' his mum asked. She retrieved a bottle of wine from the fridge and held it up—a second unspoken question.

'Yes, to the wine,' he said, 'and I'm not sure about the memories. Not yet.' So far the house didn't feel at all as he'd expected.

Conversation moved on as Seb's dad set the table

and Seb and his mother stood together by the stove as the salmon sizzled and spat. They talked about Seb's new business, about his parents' travel plans, the baby news of someone Seb had once gone to school with who Monique had bumped into at the supermarket...

Why had he come here? Why tonight, after he'd avoided it for so long?

Earlier, beside his car, Steph had been all he'd been able to think about. He'd expected to step inside the front door and for the emotion to be overwhelming: for the walls and floors to release his memories, for that familiar wave of grief to drown him again.

But it hadn't happened.

It had been five days since he'd seen Mila—since she'd silently exited his apartment without even a goodbye. Instead she'd left the briefest of notes.

We can't be friends any more.

That had been it.

It hadn't been unexpected—after all, that had been her response after their kiss. And their night together had been so much more. More...*everything*.

But at the time he'd hoped that *'I just want to-*

night' meant that the next morning they'd return to their regular friendship.

Or maybe that was just what he'd told himself to justify something he'd known was a truly terrible idea.

But—regardless—Seb still thought Mila's decision made no sense. Even less so now than after their kiss. Before, she'd argued that his attempts to reinvigorate their friendship were pointless because they'd both—according to Mila—neglected it for far too long. But surely the past few weeks had proved her theory wrong?

His attempts to contact her to discover the real problem had proved fruitless. She'd simply repeated her note, with slight variations, in her text messages, or simply not answered his calls at all.

It was frustrating.

But mostly it hurt like hell.

He missed Mila.

So for five days he'd worked like a man possessed—both in the Heliotrope offices and on site. Although not at the shop beside Mila's—instinctively he knew that now was not the time to push her. After nearly twenty-five years of friendship he at least knew that.

What he *didn't* know was how he felt about that night, aside from the fact it had led to Mila's removal from his life. He wasn't allowing himself to think about it—and his extreme work habits had allowed him to achieve that goal.

His priority was somehow getting Mila back in his life. That was all that mattered.

He looked down at his plate. He'd cleared it of every morsel, but had no recollection of actually eating it.

'Dessert?' his mum asked.

He nodded.

So why come here tonight? To this house chock full of memories of Steph *and* of Mila? With every minute he was here—and with every disjointed thought that careened through his brain—it became clearer to him that it was not a coincidence.

He'd been wary of this place for so long. Wary of the pain he was so sure it would trigger. But he'd been wrong. In this house he felt comforted by history. By memories of giggling games of hide and seek and bowls of salty popcorn in front of the VCR.

Was that it? After five days without Mila he wanted to be near her—no matter how obliquely?

No. Not even close.

Finally he realised this had nothing to do with Mila.

This had everything to do with Steph.

Slowly he tuned back in to the conversation. His mum served up a still steaming apple pie, placing perfect little scoops of vanilla bean ice cream beside each piece.

'Did you see it?' his mum asked.

Belatedly Seb realised she was talking to him.

'Pardon me?'

'The photo in that magazine. You know—the one that comes in the weekend paper.' She paused as she pressed the lid back onto the ice cream carton. 'The photo of you and Mila Molyneux. At a film premiere.'

'I didn't know you were seeing her,' said his dad. 'I've always liked her—a straight talker, that girl.'

'She does something crafty now,' his mum said, all conversationally. 'Pots, is it?'

Seb shoved back his seat, needing to stand up. 'I'm not seeing her,' he said.

But once he was standing he had no further plan. Just for something to do, he grabbed his empty wine glass and put it in the dishwasher.

Ah. *This* was it. This feeling when his parents mentioned Mila. That little leap in his pulse, the instant flashback to memories he'd not allowed himself to reflect upon.

That was why he wanted to come here tonight. That was why he'd wanted to feel close to Steph...

Because Mila wasn't like the women he'd slept with in London.

Mila wasn't the first woman he'd slept with after Steph, but she was the first who mattered.

He didn't feel guilty—as if he'd cheated on Steph or anything. But it did feel significant. As significant as the day he'd stopped wearing his wedding band.

Does this mean I'm really moving on, Steph?

And was that also why he'd embargoed his own memories of that night? Had he hoped, somehow, that Mila *had* been like the others? Out of some form of misplaced loyalty to Steph?

Possibly. But that was stupid.

Had he hoped that because then it would be easy? Then he could easily argue to Mila that it had just been a bit of meaningless fun and there was no reason why their friendship couldn't go straight back to the way it had been.

She was the first one who mattered. What did that even mean?

Seb had walked back to the table now and he ate his pie mindlessly, watching his ice cream become a puddle.

After dessert he stood up again. This time he ended up at the window. Outside it was now dark, the tall trees that lined the rear fence merging into the black sky.

'Honey, is there anything you want to talk about?'

His mum's voice was gentle, her tone reassuring.

Seb ran his hands through his hair. 'No.'

This definitely wasn't something he wanted to share with his parents: his brain full of Steph and Mila and messy confusion. He didn't want to share it with anybody. He wasn't good at talking about this stuff.

After Steph's death he'd had his PA back at Fyfe Technology find him a counsellor to talk to—it had seemed the sensible thing to do. What he would have organised for any member of his staff.

Besides, he'd hardly had other options. With Steph's death had come an ugly truth: not only had he not truly known his wife any more, but he was surrounded by a crowd of people who either worked for him or were nothing but the most superficial of acquaintances. His work had become his wife, his friend, his family.

He'd had nobody to talk to—except maybe his parents. And, as desperate as they'd been to help, he just hadn't been capable of revealing how pathetic he was, how little he'd known about the woman he'd once loved.

There'd been Mila, too—with her regular and then more intermittent emails and social media messages. She'd been the only one who'd persisted for more than a few weeks—she tried for months until he'd eventually driven her away with his calculated rudeness.

But he just hadn't been able to talk to her—not then.

He'd been broken, grief-stricken.

Ashamed.

So he'd gone to the counsellor his PA had booked. He'd sat in the waiting room. And then left without seeing her.

In the end, talking had seemed impossible. So he'd remained alone and silent.

Eventually—and it had come gradually, with no epiphany or any particular day he could remember—he hadn't wanted to be alone any more. So he'd sold Fyfe, despite its success, because of all it had represented and reminded him of. His flaws, his mistakes, those wasted years.

And he'd come home to be close to those who still truly cared for him. His parents. Mila.

One night *could not* be the end of his friendship with Mila.

It could *not*.

He pushed open the sliding door and stepped out

onto the deck. A few metres away was the glass pool fence, twinkling in the light reflected from the house. It was cool, but still, outside.

Seb had walked a few steps when he heard movement behind him. He looked over his shoulder—his father had slid the door shut and, with a nod, left Seb alone.

To his right was the pool house, and it felt natural that Seb went there. The wooden bi-fold doors that made up two of the walls were pushed partly open, so Seb opened one of them the rest of the way, before collapsing onto a large day bed, his legs stretched out before him.

For a long while he just lay there, staring at the raked ceiling. He didn't really understand what he was doing, or what he was thinking. Out here—more so than in the house—snippets of memories whizzed through his brain. Most were almost too quick to grasp—vignettes of a primary school age birthday party, Christmas lunches his parents had hosted, water bomb competitions off the diving board.

But others lingered: Mila suggesting they jump off his mum's exercise trampoline and into the pool. Steph claiming she could hold her breath underwater *'waaaayyy'* longer than Seb could. The afternoons they'd been supposed to study together but had instead sprawled in the pool house, discussing everything and anything—with the earnestness and intensity of teenagers who thought they knew it all.

In the end calling Mila seemed the only possible thing to do.

She didn't answer his first call, but she picked up after what seemed like infinite rings on his second.

'I told you, Seb—'

'I'm at the pool house,' Seb said, interrupting. 'Can you come over?'

Saying no hadn't been an option.

In fact it hadn't even been a consideration. Which should've been weird, given Mila had literally been in the process of telling Seb never to contact her again when he'd asked her.

But it was the pool house. *The pool house.*

So she'd come straight over. After a quick visit to the bottle shop.

Monique and Kevin had simply ushered her through when she'd arrived.

She wore jeans and a singlet, and her flip flops were loud against the merbau decking, the evening air cool against her skin.

Seb was sprawled across the day bed in almost

darkness, the pool house lit only by the light from the main house.

'I brought your favourite,' Mila called out.

He propped himself up on one elbow as she approached. 'You drink schnapps?' he asked, incredulous.

'Only on special occasions,' Mila said, handing him the bottle.

She walked over to the small bar that still occupied the corner of the pool house. In the limited light she grabbed a couple of shot glasses, and noted that the alcohol was no longer locked away in some undisclosed location in Seb's house. Instead the bottles lined a couple of shelves along the wall, no longer vulnerable to curious teenagers. No peach schnapps, though.

Seb pulled himself up, propping his back against the plush cushions that edged the day bed. Mila crawled across the mattress to sit beside him. But not touching.

Seb was staring straight ahead, across the pool. Silently, she handed the glasses to him and then poured them both a drink.

'Why did you invite me over?' Mila asked, then immediately downed her drink.

Seb followed her lead, then grimaced. 'How on earth did we drink a bottle of this?'

'Why did you invite me over?' Mila repeated, ignoring him.

Seb finally held her gaze. She could tell he was, despite the darkness, simply by the intensity of him doing so.

Now that her eyes had adjusted to the mix of moon and ambient light she could make out more details of his face: a few days' worth of stubble on his jaw, lines of tension etched about his eyes and mouth.

'I need to talk,' he said. 'About Steph.' He swallowed. 'I want you to talk about Steph, too.'

The request was not unexpected, Mila knew the significance of the pool house. Knew the hundreds of memories the three of them had shared here. And of course knew the memories that should have been between only Seb and Steph.

She'd been Steph's best friend and they'd been seventeen. She *knew* Steph had lost her virginity here. She knew more details than she'd probably needed to—but then, she'd been seventeen and curious too.

Back then she'd felt occasional flutters of jealousy—she'd carried a little torch for Seb through numerous boyfriends of her own. But she'd simply boxed up her crush, not allowing it to impact on her friendship with Steph or with Seb. It had been simply what it was. Nothing more. She'd been happy for them both.

But now, only days after sleeping naked beside this man...days since he'd been inside her...it was hard. To be here beside this man and beside the memory of Steph.

'Mila?'

At some point her gaze had dropped to her hands. She'd knotted her fingers together, but now she disentangled them, laying her hands flat against her thighs.

But wasn't *all* of this hard? For both of them? She'd known that when Seb had asked her to come here. She'd known what she was doing, and she'd also known she needed to do it.

For Seb and for herself.

'When we were thirteen, I dared Steph to steal a bottle of purple glitter nail polish from that chemist near Teli's Deli. Remember it?'

Mila looked up, at Seb watching her. He nodded.

'I never thought she'd do it, but she did. No one noticed...no one knew. For about five minutes we thought we were the biggest, coolest rebels ever. And then we felt terrible. Steph started crying.'

Mila's lips quirked upwards. She was remembering how they'd sat under the shade of a Moreton

Bay Fig at a park nearby, their ill-gotten contra-band lying on the grass between them.

'Then I started crying too, and we ended up going home and telling Ivy. Ivy made us go back to the chemist, tell the manager what we did, and pay for it. She never told our parents, never told anyone. We didn't tell anyone, either.'

'Not even me?'

Mila shook her head. 'No.'

Seb smiled. 'Steph told me that story.'

'No!' Mila said, genuinely shocked. 'We had a *pact*!' She said it with all the latent indignation of her thirteen-year-old self.

He shrugged. 'We'd had too much to drink at a party in London one night. I can't remember why it came up. She made me promise never to tell you I knew, and she was mortified she'd told me.' He smiled. 'But I always did wonder—why didn't you tell me back then?'

'There were always some things that were just between Steph and me.'

For a while they sat in silence. Long enough for Mila to tune in to the sounds around them: the regular chirp of crickets, hidden somewhere in the lush gardens, Rustling leaves. And, further away, the muffled sounds of the occasional car travel-ling down the street.

'Did she tell you about us?' Seb said, then cleared his throat. 'That she wasn't happy?'

Automatically Mila went to shake her head—but then she realised that a denial would not be entirely truthful. 'We didn't speak often over the past few years,' she said. She'd do anything to turn back time and change that. 'But when we did we used to talk for hours. She'd talk about her business, about where you were living, about all the new people she was meeting. And about you. A lot. She was so proud of your success.'

Mila paused. Although they sat side by side Mila was looking straight ahead, her gaze focused on the perfect glass-like surface of the pool.

'But our conversations became shorter as they became further apart. And I started to notice that I had to ask about you. You didn't seem to be such a large part of the life that she was sharing with me. I noticed that, but I didn't question it.'

'Why not?' Seb asked, but with only curiosity, not censure.

'Because she sounded happy. Maybe I thought she would mention it herself if there was a problem—or a problem she wanted me to know about.' Now Mila turned towards Seb, tucking her legs beneath her. 'I guess that says a lot about how our relationship changed. I was only sharing the high-lights of *my* life, too. Not the messy bits.'

Seb just watched silently as she spoke, his expression unreadable.

'But mostly,' Mila said, 'I don't think I really believed it. I mean—you were both so happy. So perfect together.'

'We were far from perfect.'

'I should've asked her—'

'You wouldn't have had anything to ask if I'd been a better husband.'

'I'm sure it wasn't all your fault,' Mila said gently.

'Based on all the conversations you had with Steph about our relationship?' His words were flat. Brutal.

'Ouch.'

Seb ran his hands through his hair. Now he was looking out at the pool. 'I'm sorry. I'm being unfair.' He sighed. 'Objective me can quote all sorts of clichés about relationships being a two-way street, or say that it takes two to tango... But I was there and I knew things were breaking—that they were broken. And I did nothing. I just went to work each day, carrying on like normal.'

'What did Steph do to try and save your relationship?'

Seb didn't like that question. It was apparent in every instantly tense line of his body.

'She tried harder than me. She tried to talk about it, but I didn't want to know. She organised counselling, but I'd always cancel.'

'Why?'

'I've asked myself that a million times,' he said, with a rough facsimile of a laugh. 'At the time it was basic denial. I just didn't want to deal with it. But obviously it was more than that. Of course I knew that it was over. But I didn't want to think about what that meant. Steph and I had set up a life together. We'd left our families behind. And we'd been more successful than in our wildest dreams. If we broke up, what would happen to the perfect life we had? If the relationship that had been core to our success failed, what did that mean for everything else? I'd been with Steph for half my life. My success seemed intrinsically tied up with hers and with *her*.' He sighed. 'So that's what it came down to. Fear of failure. Pretty pathetic, huh?'

Mila didn't say a word, just allowed Seb's words to keep on flowing.

'When I noticed how much she was going out, how many nights she'd get home at crazy hours, I did ask what she was doing, but she assured me all was well. I knew it wasn't, but she was still going to work each day, her business was still doing so well...' He shook his head. 'What does that say about me? That I'd use capability for work as an indicator she was okay? Part of me knew it was destructive behaviour, knew that we were in the death throes of our marriage. I think she knew, too. But we were both just too busy to get around to ending it, to dealing with the end of Stephanie and Sebastian. It seemed impossible.'

He swallowed.

'I think she might have been seeing someone, actually. We had a memorial service in London, and there were a group of friends there I didn't recognise. I hated them instantly, because I associated them with what her life had become—the parties, the drugs. But they weren't what I expected—they looked like professionals. Young, financially secure. Which made sense. Steph overdosed in a penthouse in South Kensington, not in a gutter.'

Mila realised she was crying. Silent tears were sliding down her cheeks and dripping from her chin.

'One guy...I don't know...I just *knew*. He wouldn't look at me. And he was pretty cut up. His friends seemed to be rallying around him.'

Mila had to touch him so she slid closer, holding his hand.

'Steph's choices were not your responsibility,' Mila said softly.

'I failed her, Mila—can't you see that?' Seb said, his words firm. 'It doesn't make any difference who introduced her to her dealer, or what happened next. All that matters is that I was supposed to be there for her—more than anyone else in the world. And I wasn't. I was distant—emotionally, geographically. I was too obsessed with my company and its continued success to make time for our relationship. I even made sure I was too busy to end our relationship—to let her move on with her life. I was selfish and I was scared. I failed her.'

Mila gripped his fingers harder. 'I failed her too,' she said. 'I wasn't the best friend I was supposed to be. I let time and time zones transform us into being little more than acquaintances, always with the best of intentions to reignite our friendship "one day".' She wiped at her eyes ineffectively, leaving her palm damp with tears. 'One day...' she repeated.

For a long while they both sat in silence, surrounded by their choices, their mistakes, their regrets.

A leaf had marred the perfect surface of the pool, and Mila watched its slow, directionless journey across the water.

'Do you remember when Steph was going to make her fortune baking Steph's special mint slice?' Seb said, after an eternity. 'How old were you? Twelve? She even made a website on one of those awful free site-builders with a never-ending web address...'

And just like that, they started talking about Steph.

CHAPTER ELEVEN

SEB WOKE TO the warmth of the sun against his skin.

It was an effort to open his eyes because his eyelids were heavy. His whole body was heavy, in fact.

It was early—early enough that the sun was still low and able to stretch its rays into the pool house. Beside him, on her side, lay Mila. She was still asleep, with yesterday's make-up slightly smudged beneath her eyes, one arm stretched out towards him. Her singlet top was twisted at her waist, revealing a strip of pale stomach above her jeans. Her feet were bare, her shoes kicked to the ground.

But she no longer touched him. At some point as they'd slept their hands had fallen apart.

Seb couldn't remember a decision to sleep in the pool house. All he remembered was the pair of them talking. Talking and talking—sharing memories of Steph. Memories of the three of them together. Memories of Steph and Seb and also of Steph and Mila.

The bottle of peach schnapps had been abandoned early on, to be replaced with a selection of other spirits from his parents' bar. The small stack of shot glasses lined up along the wooden back of the day bed perfectly explained his lethargy, as well as the fogginess of his brain.

'Morning,' said Mila, her lovely eyes blinking at Seb sleepily.

He smiled. 'Good morning,' he replied—and it was. A *really* good morning, he decided. Today, despite the after-effects of alcohol, he felt good. Really good.

'I guess all those people telling me I needed to talk about Steph were on to something.'

Mila laughed, the sound startling a small honeyeater perched on the glass pool fence. It flew away in a flurry of flapping wings. 'Talking *is* good,' she agreed. 'I did a lot of talking early on—to Ivy especially. She's a good listener.'

'I'm sorry I was so awful to you back then,' he said. 'You wanted to talk and I wouldn't let you.'

'Yeah...' Mila said, all matter-of-fact. 'Desperately. But maybe waiting wasn't so bad. I wasn't ready to talk about the good times straight after Steph died.'

And that was what they'd done. Once they'd laid all their guilt out on the table they'd simply reminisced together. Sharing everything and anything that included Steph, and nearly every story and anecdote had led to laughter.

That was what had changed in Seb last night. For the first time since Steph's death Seb had smiled as he'd remembered her. Together he and Mila had celebrated Steph, without allowing the shackles of grief and regret to weigh them down.

He *was* moving on. He believed that now.

Together they walked inside to the empty kitchen. His parents were nowhere to be seen, and a scribbled note on the counter indicated they'd headed out for breakfast.

The time on the microwave revealed it was really time to get to work, but they both seemed comfortable in their sluggishness. Without asking, Seb poured them both a long glass of water, and they stood, not so far apart, staring out at the garden as they drank.

Later they headed for their cars. They'd still barely spoken. Mila pressed the button on her key to unlock her car, and it did so with a definite *thunk*.

'Thank you,' Seb said, stepping closer to Mila.

She smiled. 'Thank *you*. I needed last night, too.'

She turned and opened the driver's side door, tossing her bag onto the passenger seat.

'So...' he said.

Mila twisted back to face him, her gaze direct. 'What happens now?' she asked.

Mila's note hung metaphorically between them: *We can't be friends any more.*

But surely that note could now be torn up and thrown away? Surely last night had shown Mila that their friendship was the furthest they could get from the *'waste of time'* she'd claimed it to be after that first kiss?

'I won't pretend to understand why you ran away on Wednesday morning.'

'I *didn't* run away...'A pause. 'Okay,' she conceded, 'maybe I did—but I thought it was the right thing to do. Because I knew what you'd say if I'd stayed.'

'That I wanted us to stay friends?'

He desperately wanted them to. He would say anything and everything to make that happen. Last night had only underlined how important Mila was to him. How irreplaceable she was. How irreplaceable their *friendship* was.

'I can't do that, Seb.'

'Pardon me?' Seb blinked, shocked to his core. 'So last night changed *nothing*?'

He couldn't believe this. How could last night mean so much to him, but nothing to her?

Mila shook her head. 'No. It changed everything.'

Seb went still.

Mila's gaze did not waver from his. 'I can't walk away from you. Not now. But I can't just be your friend. I can't pretend any more.'

This was not what he'd expected.

'I lied,' she continued. 'When you asked me whether I wanted you to kiss me at the beach. I *did* want you to kiss me. I just hadn't admitted it to myself yet. But I did. Maybe from the moment you stepped back into my life.' Half a smile. 'I don't want to lie to myself any more.'

Seb didn't know what to think. His brain, his heart, his pulse—everything—was ratcheting every which way.

'I wanted that kiss, too,' he said. Now was not the time for the subterfuge that Mila had once said she hated. 'I wanted *you*,' he clarified.

'Wanted?' she prompted.

'*Want,*' he said, running a hand through his hair, frustrated, because of course that was true. He wanted Mila. 'But I was hoping to manage that. For the sake of our friendship I thought I could withstand a bit of sexual tension—'

Mila laughed out loud.

He knew it sounded ridiculous. But he didn't know how else to deal with this. Of any other way to cope.

'I didn't expect this,' he said. 'I wanted our friendship back. Nothing more.'

Mila laughed again, this time high-pitched. 'And you think this is what *I* want?'

'What *do* you want?' Seb asked.

There was the slightest wobble to her gaze. Subtle, but there.

'I don't want to pretend around you,' she said. 'That's all I know.'

'I don't want to hurt you. And I don't want to lose you. And I have no idea how to stop both those things happening if we're anything more than friends.'

Abruptly, Mila climbed into her seat, calmly clicking her seat belt into place. 'We're *not* just friends, Seb,' she said, her words sharp. 'How can you say you want me in one breath and try to talk me into remaining your friend in the next?'

'We did it before—after that kiss,' he said, stubbornly refusing to concede. 'Why can't we do it again?'

Mila shook her head, breathing an angry, frustrated sigh. She reached for the door, to pull it shut.

He could have held the door, forced her to keep it open, but what would that have achieved?

So instead he dropped to his haunches, laying his hand over hers. They'd spent most of the night holding hands. As friends, then, nothing more.

He'd hoped maybe by touching her now that he could prove his point. That they could put Tuesday night behind them. That he could show her how the electricity between them had abated.

As his fingers brushed her skin he realised how very wrong he was.

His gaze shot up, tangling with hers.

'No, we're not just friends,' he repeated.

He crouched between the partially open door and Mila. Her hand had fallen away from the door handle and he held it in both of his.

Outside of the sanctuary of the pool house—outside of that bubble they'd created for their memories—they were right back where they'd started. Right where they'd been since he'd walked into Mila's shop that very first evening.

Sensation shot between them where they touched. His body's reaction was visceral, needing her, wanting her.

No. He was too selfish. Too damaged. And Mila was too fragile. Ben, her dad…their appalling behaviour was still so fresh…

But all that made no difference. *Yes* was all his body could say.

Mila was looking away, out through the windscreen. 'I know you said you weren't ready for a relationship,' she said. 'And I don't think I'm ready either.'

Seb still held her hand. He ran his thumb along her palm, then loosely traced the shape of her fingers.

'So where does that leave us?' she continued, her words soft and breathy. 'Not friends. Not a relationship.'

'Does it matter?' Seb said. 'How about we just focus on not being friends for a while.'

'Not being friends?' She smiled. 'I like that.' Mila reached out again for the door handle. 'But I really have to get to work. My shop is supposed to open in—'

Seb silenced her with a kiss.

Ivy was working at the office today, so she arrived at the small café near April's place in her chauffeur-driven car.

Mila had arrived first, so she watched Ivy approach from her seat in the small booth she'd chosen at the rear of the café. Every person eating there watched her sister approach—people always did. Ivy had such an air of confidence and authority that she just drew people to her.

Today she wore one of her typically sharp work outfits—black cigarette pants with red-soled black pumps, cream sleeveless blouse tucked in neatly, and oversized Hollywood sunglasses. She looked exactly like the billion-odd dollars she was worth.

Ivy smiled as she spotted Mila, and whipped off her sunglasses. Her sister hurried over, completely unaware that she was the centre of attention. Mila smiled—her sister was definitely the most down-to-earth billionaire on the planet. Just one of the several hundred reasons Mila loved her.

She'd invited Ivy and April to lunch on a whim. The past week had been just...*so much*. Too much to process. Really, everything that had happened since she'd had that taxi drop her off at Seb's apartment building had been intense.

She needed her sisters.

Ivy slid into the booth beside Mila and together they perused the menu. April was always late, but she did manage to turn up only a few minutes past twelve. She glided into the café, the total antithesis of efficient, focused Ivy.

Today she was very much Boho, with her long blonde hair in loose curls that cascaded over the thin straps of her pale pink maxi-dress and the collection of fine gold necklaces that decorated the deep V of her bodice. But even dressed casually, April looked as if she'd walked off the pages of a magazine. Not that such a polished, perfect appearance came without effort, despite her sister's natural gorgeousness. Especially now that April traded so heavily on her appearance.

'Apologies!' April said, by way of a greeting. 'I have no perception of time. Hey—can I get the annoying selfie request out of the way? Mila, I'll tag your shop—it's sure to drive a few more sales. People went nuts for those concrete vase things the other week.'

'Molyneux Mining doesn't do social media,' pointed out Ivy. 'Or have any need to drum up business.'

'Nope,' April said cheerfully. 'But everyone loves a photo of Ivy Molyneux acting like a normal human being. I'm sure your marketing people have worked out how much your customer whatsit scores improved after you were papped with Nate at the supermarket.'

'You know,' Ivy said, 'reminding me of the time I was photographed without make-up and with baby spew on my shoulder is probably *not* the best way to convince me of anything.'

'*Pfft!*' said April. 'You always look beautiful.

Plus you had a six-foot-four commando pushing your trolley. All anyone was thinking was, *Phwoar!*'

Ivy looked at Mila. 'I'm really not sure I'm following our sister's argument.'

'Just let her take the picture,' Mila advised. 'Then we'll get to eat.'

A few minutes of posing, and judicious application of filters, and April was happily hashtagging away while Mila went to order for them all at the counter.

She watched her sisters chatting as she waited in the queue. They were both so different—from each other and from Mila. Mila had always thought she was more like Ivy—more through process of elimination rather than any obvious similarities. Mila's view of life just seemed to have more of an acerbic edge than April's, and she guessed she identified with Ivy's more serious personality. But she was equally close to them both. April's sunniness and optimism were contagious, while Ivy could always be relied on for her wisdom—even if it was not always requested.

But Mila knew she wasn't going to tell them about Seb today.

It wasn't like her not to tell her sisters about men

she was dating. It wasn't like her not to tell them about *anything*. It was just...she wasn't dating Seb.

What they had was too intangible. Heck, if she and Seb couldn't even give it a name what was there to tell anyone, anyway? That she and Seb *weren't* friends any more? But that they also weren't quite anything else?

No. It was definitely better to say nothing.

At the front of the queue, Mila ordered efficiently, then collected a frosty bottle of water and three small tumblers. Back at the table she poured them all a glass of water, then fell into the deep red padded seat of the booth. All her muscles ached—her body was remembering exactly how much she'd drunk last night, and how late she'd been up talking.

Eventually she realised her sisters were talking about their dad.

'I couldn't believe it,' Ivy was saying, 'when my assistant told me. It's been *years.*'

'What did he want?'

Ivy shrugged. 'I have no idea. I didn't return his calls.'

'Me either,' April said. 'Do you know he's finally worked out social media? His accounts are following all mine now. I did consider blocking him, but it seemed pretty petty when I share my photos and ramblings with literally everyone else in the universe.'

'I blocked him,' Mila said quietly. 'And my business accounts don't even have enough followers that I can really afford to do that.'

Blaine had called her, too, but there'd been no chance of her answering.

'So that's it, then?' Ivy asked. 'You're done?'

Mila nodded. 'Yes. *So* done. No more chances.'

'You sure?' April asked, looking over the top of her water glass.

Mila raised her eyebrows. 'Really?' she said. 'I thought you'd be overjoyed.'

'I am,' Ivy said firmly.

April rolled her eyes. 'I just wanted to make sure this was *your* decision. Not ours. Because it's a big one.'

Mila nodded. 'I get it. But, no—this one was definitely *all* on Blaine. Although—just so it's noted—you were both absolutely right. I should've stopped answering his calls years ago.'

She'd given Ivy and April a condensed version of her night at the film premiere—with the beach scene with Seb completely removed.

'Of course,' Ivy said with a grin.

Their lunches arrived, and Mila sat back in the booth as the waiter organised their food on the table. She'd ordered gnocchi, with a chunky tomato sauce piled on top.

Her sisters were sharing anecdotes about their dad. Each demonstrated his uselessness perfectly, and each, with the benefit of time, had become humorous. All of Blaine's failures preceded with a dramatic, *'And then he—'*

She smiled along with them, but wasn't really paying attention. Instead, all she could think about was Seb.

Had she done the right thing?

She was so confused. She'd thought she'd already dealt with this. The morning she'd walked out of Seb's apartment she'd thought she'd walked out of his life.

Last night, in the pool house, had been important. She was glad she'd followed her instincts when he'd called—glad she'd been there with him. Both for Seb and for herself. For the first time since Stephanie's death she'd laughed as she'd thought about her. Smiled as she'd remembered the girl, and the woman, who had been such a significant part of her life.

So that had been good. Great. But after...? Outside Seb's parents' house...?

She'd followed her gut once again—followed an almost primeval need to be authentic, to refuse to accept Seb's faux friendship, but this time also to refuse to deny the pull she felt to Seb.

When he touched her she could think of nothing else but him—the sensation of his hands against her skin was electric, compelling, addictive.

With Seb, whenever she was with him, it had just always felt *right*. And that, in itself, made her uncomfortable.

Because even *rightness* seemed an unlikely concept—too similar to her habit of manufacturing pretty delusions, like her fanciful hopes with her dad, rather than facing reality. It certainly wasn't something she could trust or rely upon as a gauge of anything real or substantial.

Mila's fork scraped against the bottom of her plate. She'd eaten most of her lunch, and now simply pushed the remaining little balls of gnocchi around in circles.

'You okay, hon?' Ivy bumped her shoulder against Mila's. 'You've been very quiet.'

It was tempting. It would be so very easy to tell them all that had happened in the past few days. She trusted them both. Completely. But she couldn't.

They'd disapproved of her persistence with their dad. They'd worried for her, and been there for her, but they'd never approved. They'd never really understood why she kept putting herself through something where the final destination was always going to be hurt and tears.

Would they think she was on the same journey now, with Seb?

He'd told her he didn't want a relationship, which Mila knew really meant that he didn't want a relationship with *her*. His words that night at the beach had made that clear: *'This is wrong...'*

It didn't get much clearer than that, despite all the supposed *rightness* she thought she felt.

She'd told herself that she'd keep an emotional distance from Seb. That this was just about a physical attraction. This was about them both each needing each other—right now—and nothing more. She wasn't ready for a relationship. She didn't even want a relationship with Seb...

And most importantly she kept telling herself that she'd learnt from what had happened with Ben, from what had happened with her dad. She was still in control. She wasn't going to get hurt.

But would Ivy and April believe that? Did *she*?

She didn't think she could face it—her sisters' concern for the naïve little sister they had to look out for.

No. She was an adult. She'd made her choice.

She had to live with it—without her big sisters holding her hand.

'I'm fine!' she said with a smile. 'Really. Okay—now, who wants to share a slice of carrot cake with me?'

CHAPTER TWELVE

SEB KNOCKED ON the back door of Mila's Nest after work. They hadn't organised for him to come over, but Mila had known he would.

Mila had been wiping down the tables in the workshop and collecting stray pieces of clay left over from her students' endeavours. Sheri had already gone home, and the *'Closed'* sign was hung on the shop's front door. She had the radio playing, and an enthusiastic voice was currently describing the peak hour traffic conditions in significant detail.

Mila took her time walking to the door. She might have known that Seb would come over, but now that he was here she wasn't entirely sure how she felt about it.

She was acutely aware of her own heartbeat, madly accelerating away within her chest. Her cheeks felt warm too, as if she could feel Seb's gaze already—irrespective of the solid wooden door separating them.

Seb knocked again just as Mila's hand grasped the door handle, making her jump.

It seemed impossible that this time yesterday she'd been convinced she'd never see Sebastian Fyfe again.

Finally she swung open the door, and then the security screen. Seb waited impatiently, his gaze distracting, exactly as intense as she'd imagined.

'Hey,' he said.

Mila stepped back, gesturing with her arm that he should come inside. As she closed the door behind them, her back to Seb as she deadbolted the door and slid the security chain into place, she wondered what to do now.

Did she invite him to stay for dinner? Did they go out somewhere for a drink? She had no idea what the protocols were for not being friends.

She pivoted to face him. 'So,' she said. 'How do you want to do this?'

'Well,' he said, reaching for her, then tugging her close. 'How about we start with a kiss?'

And just like that his mouth was on hers, and Mila was incapable of thinking about anything but how good that felt.

She kissed him back as she drew him closer, twining her hands around his neck and her fingers in his hair. His hands were firm against her:

at the small of her back and at her waist. Her T-shirt had ridden up, just a little, and when his hand touched her skin her belly flooded with warmth. But it wasn't nearly enough—she needed more. She was greedy for it.

There was a thunking sound as Seb's back hit the closed door behind him, and he smiled against Mila's mouth. She smiled right back as he moved her, and then she was the one against the door. Seb's shoulders—his height—boxed her in, but it was a delicious sensation...the sense of Seb's power, his passion—he wanted her. And of course she was an equal in this. She wanted him just as desperately—with her own touch: her mouth, her hands, she was just as powerful.

There was a freedom to this kiss. This was a kiss where there would be another. This wasn't a one-time chance. This wasn't a spur-of-the-moment decision.

Because Mila didn't just have Seb for tonight. She had him until...

Until when?

Beyond tomorrow, yes—but how long after that? Days, weeks, months? Until she wanted to end it? Or until Seb did?

Seb went still, his lips against Mila's neck.

'You're thinking too much,' he said, his breath hot against her skin. 'Is something wrong?'

She shook her head, then slid her hands beneath his shirt. His stomach was firm, his belt a hard edge beneath her palm.

'No,' she said. Firmly. Because nothing was wrong—and nothing *would* be wrong. Unwanted thoughts of the future just fed into her old habits and unreliable hopes and dreams.

All she needed to worry about was right now. Not tomorrow, next week or next month. And right now only one thing was important to her.

'Kiss me again,' she said.

And he did—many more times than once—then followed Mila up the stairs to her apartment, holding her hand.

On Tuesday, Seb brought Mila lunch. She was busy with customers and classes, and he had a meeting to get to—but still he brought her lunch. He'd said he would, and he did—and that made Mila smile as she watched him stride from her shop, her gaze admiring the broadness of his shoulders.

Later, they ate fish and chips on Cottesloe Beach. Stealthy seagulls hovered just beyond the unravelled butcher's paper packaging, and the sea breeze blew Mila's hair in every direction.

They ate in the next evening, out on the balcony at Seb's place. The views across to the river were spectacular as they cradled crusty bread rolls filled with chevups, barbecued onions and tomato sauce.

The next night was Mila's monthly dinner with her mum and her sisters. Again, she didn't mention Seb—but this time, she did so with confidence.

At lunch at that café, she'd second guessed her decision, unused to keeping secrets from her sisters. But now, it just made sense.

She'd told Seb weeks ago that she hadn't yet worked out how to protect herself from getting hurt, but keeping their not-a-relationship secret felt like part of it. It was all part of keeping an emotional distance—of not imagining more than there actually was.

As soon as they told people expectations would be created. By others. By herself.

And without expectations, Mila was simply enjoying herself.

Really—if she thought about it—wasn't it *better* that she didn't leap back into a relationship after what had happened with Ben? Wasn't just relaxing and having a bit of fun a *good* thing?

And this thing with Seb was definitely *good*. She couldn't remember feeling this way before—all fluttery and displaced whenever she was around him. Or even when she thought of him. It hadn't been like that with Ben. Mila didn't know what it was. Maybe the remnants of her heart-pounding, hormone-infused teenage crush?

It must be, she decided.

And so—once again—she didn't breathe a word about Seb.

On Sunday, Seb and Mila sat side by side at one of the benches in Mila's workshop.

It wasn't too early—they'd both slept in, waking up tangled in Mila's sheets.

Seb had headed out in search of coffee and croissants, and now he tore off pieces of pastry from within a brown paper bag as he listened to Mila's instructions.

He'd asked, last night, about her classes, curious to know how her business had evolved. It hadn't surprised him at all to learn it had begun with a challenge: Ivy had proclaimed herself lacking any artistic ability, and the challenge had been on.

'To be honest,' Mila had said, 'she made a pretty awful little pot. But we had fun, and the idea just went from there. Most of my students haven't done anything arty since high school.' Somehow she'd convinced him to have a go himself. 'Don't

stress,' she'd assured him, 'you're exactly my de-
mographic.'

So here they were: a pair of Lazy Susans sitting
before them, a small circle of clay placed in the
centre of each.

'Right,' Mila said. 'Now we've got the bases
done, we've got to start rolling out our coils.' She
handed Seb a lump of clay. 'Roll away.'

Seb dutifully followed Mila's instructions as
she explained the technique they were using. 'You
probably remember this from school—and maybe
pinch pots, as well?'

Seb nodded as Mila showed him how to score
the top of the long sausage he'd rolled out with a
pen-shaped wooden tool she called a needle.

'In my adult classes we always start with these
hand-building techniques before we move on to
the wheel. Anyone can master them, and it gives
everyone a bit of confidence as they're getting
started. The kids love it too, and I love the wonk-
iness of their coils, the gaps they often leave between layers.'

Seb watched as Mila quickly rolled out her own
coil, and then scored both the sausage and the circle of clay on her Lazy Susan. She then handed
the needle to Seb, so he could score his own base.

'Now, we need just a little bit of water,' she said,

dipping her fingers in the small bowl between them. She rubbed her fingers over the scored surfaces, returning for more water as needed. 'Then we join the coil to the base, using our thumbs to blend the clay.'

Seb followed Mila's instructions and soon they were both busily building their own pots, quietly rolling, scoring and stacking.

'You're very patient,' Seb said.

Mila smiled. 'That's a learned skill. Particularly with the kids. It used to be so tempting to take over and fix their mistakes. Now I know just to sit back and let them form their own creations.'

She was smoothing the outside of her pot with a rubber paddle, merging each coil into its neighbour.

Seb had finished his pot, too. It had ended up squatter than Mila's, with a wide mouth and a lopsidedness that he hadn't intended.

Mila transported both their pots to the kiln, Seb's little odd pot in stark contrast to Mila's pot of sleek perfection.

'It seems a waste of clay,' Seb said, looking at them both on the kiln shelves. 'You could make a much nicer pot out of it.'

'No!' Mila said, appalled. 'Don't say that. It's perfect.'

It really wasn't. Impulsively, he kissed her. Hard. 'What was that for?'

He met her gaze as they broke apart. 'For teaching me pottery.'

Mila eyes sparkled. 'Coil pots were on your bucket list?'

"Not quite," he said, and shoved his hands into his pockets, trying to explain. 'It's just—I've never seen you work before, or teach. This all happened while I've been away.' It was weird, really. Rather than highlighting how far they'd drifted apart in the past six years, Mila's pottery lesson instead seemed to fill in gaps—and draw them closer. 'You're really good at this.'

Mila's smile was wide. 'Thank you. So—you'll be signing up for my 8 week adult beginner's class, then?'

'No,' Seb said. Firmly.

And Mila burst into laughter.

CHAPTER THIRTEEN

THEY'D FALLEN ASLEEP in front of the TV. Seb was stretched across Mila's sofa, with Mila sprawled over him. His arm beneath her was numb, and his neck ached from the odd angle it was resting in against the arm of the sofa.

The series they'd been watching had stopped streaming, and the screen was politely asking if they were still there. But Seb couldn't quite reach his phone or the TV remote, so the question remained unanswered. He considered waking Mila. Her head was nestled against his shoulder, her dark hair tickling his jaw.

Her bed would be much more comfortable.

But Mila slept so peacefully, her breathing slow and regular, her long eyelashes fanning her cheeks.

It had been more than two weeks now, since they'd been 'not just friends'. They'd spent nearly every night together, and all day at the weekends.

It should have felt intense. Overwhelming, even. But it didn't.

Instead it felt completely natural. The obvious thing to do.

It also felt like a lot more than their admittedly silly construct of 'not just friends'. It felt like a relationship.

During the day he didn't let his thoughts drift in that direction. During the day, the concept was unwelcome. During the day he knew all the reasons why he couldn't commit to something more with Mila.

But at times like this—in the silence, while he lay beside a sleeping Mila—he questioned why that was. Because in the silence their being together felt easy. It felt right. It didn't feel complicated, or rife with difficult emotions and unavoidable hurt and disappointment.

At these times Seb had to remind himself who he was, and who Mila was. Remind himself that Mila deserved more than a man incapable of truly engaging in a relationship. Of being there for his partner. Of giving her the love that she deserved.

But lying here, in the silence, with Mila in his arms...

So, no, he didn't wake her.

Instead he ignored his aches and discomfort and held her closer—listening to the rhythm of her breathing, of her sleep, and of her dreams.

* * *

He must have carried her to bed, Mila realised.

She stretched luxuriously across the mattress, her outstretched fingertips brushing the vintage cast-iron bedhead. She was still dressed in the T-shirt she'd worn last night; her jeans were in a puddle on the carpet.

Or maybe she'd been so tired she didn't remember Seb waking her. She rolled onto her side, tugging the sheets with her. Seb slept soundly beside her, flat on his back, wearing only a pair of navy blue boxer shorts, just visible above the sheet. One arm rested by his head, the other by his side, his hand flat on his belly.

With her gaze she explored all the muscles she still wasn't quite used to. The hardness of his body—he was all angles and solid surfaces. No softness. He looked incredibly strong.

His eyes slid open. 'Hey,' he said, all sleepily. 'I could feel you looking at me.'

'I was,' Mila said, with a smile.

'And what were you thinking?'

'Whether you carried me to bed.'

Seb had turned onto his side now, to face her, the sheet falling way past his hips as he did so. 'It would be more romantic if I had, right?'

'Of course,' Mila said.

'Then,' he said, leaning closer, 'I did.'

He kissed her, and for long, long minutes Mila was lost in the miracle of his kiss.

When they finally broke apart he grinned. 'Just for full disclosure, you also did not drool on my shoulder during episode seven.'

Mila shoved him in the shoulder. 'I do *not* drool!'

'Who said you did?' said Seb, eyes twinkling, and then somehow Mila had rolled on top of him, and they were kissing each other hard, and soft, and thoroughly, until the remainder of their clothing also hit the floor.

Later, Mila rested her head on his chest, Seb's arm snug beneath her breasts.

'If you want,' Seb said very softly, his breath tickling her ear, 'I'll carry you to bed tonight. Every night, actually, if you like.'

And for some reason those words made Mila smile, and also made her eyes sting with tears.

Suddenly this all just felt *too* good. *Too* perfect.

She lifted his arm off her and wriggled away and out of bed. He looked at her, confused.

'Where you going?'

'Breakfast!' she said, with probably too much enthusiasm. 'What would you like?'

* * *

Usually on a Tuesday afternoon Mila worked alone in her workshop. Sheri manned the shop, and Mila sat at her pottery wheel and created.

Today she once again sat beside Seb at a workbench, their now fired coil pots before them, both currently the unadulterated off-white of the clay. Seb had called earlier—he'd had an afternoon meeting cancelled. She'd invited him over without hesitation, and had kissed him the moment she'd opened the workshop door, equally so.

She did wonder when this would wear off. The little rush of butterflies in her stomach whenever she saw Seb. Or when he texted her. Or when her phone rang and his name came up on the screen.

Part of her wanted it to. Because without these tingles and this excitement—this would end. There would be no more unspoken questions about what they were really doing or how long it would last. She would no longer have to halt her traitorous imagination which was so irresponsibly extrapolating their current closeness into plans for the future. A future with many more nights and weekends with Seb.

And that was unwise. Because there were no expectations between them.

She knew that, and she had to remember that. She had to learn from her past mistakes.

Seb had picked up his slightly wonky pot, and was carefully sanding away any imperfections, exactly as Mila had instructed. She leant towards him, balancing her hand on his jeans-clad thigh, and kissed his cheek. Immediately Seb placed his pot back on the table—without much care—and kissed her back on the mouth, quite thoroughly.

'Now, *this*,' Seb said, his voice rough against her ear, 'is a very interesting lesson...'

'Oh, good!' Mila said, leaning back and away from him, hiding her smile. She turned back to the pots and materials in front of them. 'It's always so exciting when my students are enthusiastic about glazes. But first—let's learn all about using a wax resist.'

Seb raised his eyebrows.

Mila picked up a small bowl filled with pale blue liquid and a foam brush. She then explained to Seb how the wax resist would prevent the glaze from gluing their pots to her kiln, and then spent some time on more decorative uses of the product.

As she applied the liquid carefully to the base of her pot Seb dragged his stool closer to hers, the wooden legs noisy against the floor. She glanced up. Seb was now so close their shoulders bumped.

'I was too far away,' he explained, his expression deliberately innocent. 'I think it's important I see every detail of this process. For my pottery education.'

Mila bit her lip so she wouldn't smile. 'I really admire your diligence.'

'Oh,' he said, leaning even closer, 'I really admire your—'

A loud knock made Mila gasp. She pushed her stool backwards, away from Seb, hard enough that it fell to the floor with a clatter.

Seb didn't move at all. Instead he simply looked up towards the open workshop door and through the locked security screen.

'Hello, Ivy,' he said simply.

With a deep breath Mila made herself calmly retrieve her fallen chair, put it back where it belonged, then turn to face her sister.

'Hi!' she said, sounding respectably close to normal. 'What a nice surprise.'

'Is it?' Ivy asked, looking confused. 'Don't we do this every week?'

From his pram, Nate gave a happy baby shout, his hands full of Ivy's mail—colourful flyers and envelopes with plastic windows.

Mila shook her head, unable to believe she'd completely forgotten about Ivy and Nate's visit.

Stupid heart-fluttering distracting tingles.

She strode to the door with a smile, unlocking the door to let Ivy and Nate in. 'Of course,' she said. 'I'm sorry. I don't know what I was thinking.'

Ivy was smiling as she pushed Nate's pram over the small doorstep. 'I could probably make a reasonable guess.'

Mila's cheeks warmed, but she didn't say a thing. Surely through the fly screen Ivy couldn't have seen too much?

Seb didn't seem to care. He walked over to kiss Ivy's cheek, then dropped down to Nate's level to smile at him.

'So,' Ivy said, 'taking some private pottery classes, then, Seb?'

Seb glanced at Mila.

She glared at him. *Don't tell Ivy.*

His forehead crinkled in confusion. 'Yes,' he said, standing up. 'I am.'

Ivy blinked. 'Oh. Should I go, then? I don't want to intrude on your lesson time.'

'You're not,' Mila interjected quickly. 'We were just finishing up.'

'Really?' Ivy said, looking at the still neat table. She knew exactly what the workshop looked like at the end of one of Mila's classes.

'It would seem so,' Seb said.

That wasn't at all helpful, and Mila shot him a pointed look. Why couldn't he just go along with this?

Instead his gaze was flat, unreadable.

'Look,' Ivy said, glancing between Mila and Seb, 'I *am* going to go.'

'Don't—' Mila began, but Ivy cut her off.

'No,' her sister said. 'I should definitely go.'

Ivy backed the pram away from Seb, then pushed it towards the door. She retrieved Mila's mail from Nate and handed it to Mila with a long, concerned look. 'You okay?' she asked, very softly.

Mila just nodded, then opened the door.

'I'll call you later,' Ivy said over her shoulder as she pushed Nate out the door.

Nate wailed in protest as they walked through the small rear courtyard and out to the access lane.

Quite firmly, Mila locked the security door, then shut the wooden door with a heavy thud. She didn't think it would work, but she tried it anyway:

'So,' Mila said with a forced smile. 'Should we get back to the wonderful world of glazing techniques?'

'No,' Seb said. 'I don't think we should.'

Mila nodded. 'I'm sorry that was a bit weird,' she said, with a deliberately casual tone.

'It *was* weird,' Seb said. 'Why?'

Seb hadn't moved, so they stood a good distance apart—Seb near the workbench, Mila beside the door.

Her instinct was to move closer to him. She didn't like being so far away, especially when he was looking at her like that—not that she could really interpret it. Disillusioned, maybe? But why?

'It's no big deal,' Mila said, attempting a nonchalant shrug. 'I just didn't want Ivy to know about us.'

She marched back towards him, dropping her mail on the workbench. Now she was closer to Seb, but he was still a few, frustrating steps away, in the middle of the workshop. She picked up a bowl of glaze, stirring it unnecessarily.

'Why not?'

'What's there to tell?' Mila said. The glaze was a murky blue colour—a shade that would magically metamorphose into an incredible vibrant purple in the kiln.

Seb crossed his arms. 'I was unaware that I was your dirty little secret.'

Mila paused in her stirring to catch his gaze. 'Now, *that* is a little dramatic,' she said.

'I don't know,' Seb said. 'You weren't at all happy to be seen with me.'

'Well,' Mila said, 'I wasn't aware that you'd been

telling everyone about us. What did your parents think when you told them you were sleeping with me?'

There was a long pause. 'I haven't told them,' he said eventually.

'Exactly!' Mila said. 'So why do you care that I haven't told my sisters?'

'Because if my parents walked into a room while you and I were talking, or flirting—or kissing, even—there is no way I would run away from you.'

It was on the tip of her tongue: *I didn't run away!* But of course she had.

'So in this hypothetical situation,' Mila said, even more defensive now, 'with you and me standing together and your parents right in front of us, what exactly would you say?'

'I don't know,' Seb said. 'I'd work it out at the time.'

Mila shook her head. 'No. You can't be all offended and up on your high horse with me and get away with that. Tell me—I want to know what you would say. How you would describe *us*.'

'It's no one's business but ours what we do,' Seb said. 'We don't need to define ourselves to anybody.'

Mila rolled her eyes. 'I'm really struggling to see how our positions are all that different.'

Seb ran his hands through his hair, his frustration obvious in every tense line of his body. 'I am aware that I'm not making the most logical argument,' he said. Then he sighed. 'All I know is that I really didn't like it when you wanted to hide us from Ivy. I really didn't.'

She hadn't liked it either, but she hadn't felt she had a choice.

Unless...

'Define *us*,' Mila said. Softly.

'Pardon me?'

At some point Mila had placed the bowl of glaze back on the table. Now she stepped close to Seb. 'If you want me to tell Ivy, and April, and everybody else in my life, then let me know what to say.' She smiled, but carefully.

'I didn't think you wanted to tell anybody?' Seb said. 'Isn't that what we're arguing about?'

He was right, but somehow Mila had moved on from that. She didn't care about Ivy right now, or what anyone thought.

Seb had said he didn't want to hide what they had. Deep down, Mila didn't either.

What did that mean?

'Define *us*,' she repeated.

He looked uncomfortable, shifting his weight from foot to foot. But in typical Seb fashion his gaze didn't falter, even as she could practically see the cogs in his brain whirring at full speed.

'I thought you were happy with this—with our...' He paused. 'With us.'

Our relationship. That was what he couldn't say.

That bothered her. And it really bothered her that it did.

'I thought I was,' she said. 'I thought we were both on the same page. It appears we're not.'

Seb shoved his hands into the pockets of his jeans. 'Can we just forget the past twenty minutes ever happened?'

'No.'

'Didn't you want to forget it had ever happened just five minutes ago?'

She shrugged. 'I changed my mind.'

There was a long silence. Seb just looked at her—*really* looked at her—as if trying to work out what she was thinking.

Which would be difficult, as she didn't really know herself.

This was too contradictory. Too confusing.

'Mila?'

She'd been quiet too long. They both had. The

silence was heavy with too much... Just too much. Too much thinking, too much everything.

'I *really* want to forget this ever happened, Mila,' Seb was saying. His lips quirked upwards. 'This is the most fun I've had in...as long as I can remember. Years.'

'Me too,' she said. She couldn't pretend otherwise.

She realised she was tangling her fingers together and pulled her hands apart, laying her palms flat against her hips.

'You know,' Mila said, 'we weren't supposed to see each other every day.'

'What do you mean?'

Mila glanced down at her scarlet-painted toes and her tan sandal straps. 'This isn't what I expected.'

'This isn't what I expected, either,' said Seb. But he didn't elaborate.

'I think I need a definition, Seb. I need to know what *this* is.'

Mila knew this was all wrong—that this went against everything she'd been telling herself—but she was completely unable to stop it.

All along she'd been telling Seb that she didn't want to lie to herself. That she didn't want to pretend. But wasn't that exactly what she was doing?

In the guise of keeping her distance? Of protecting herself?

She lifted her gaze, meeting his. Waiting.

'What *are* we, Seb?' she prompted.

'We're good,' he said, his voice a little rough. 'We're right. Things feel right when I'm with you.'

'And?' she prompted. They were nice words, but they didn't actually mean anything.

He was looking at her so intensely, looking right inside her.

'That's it,' he said. 'That's all I can offer.'

Nothing had changed.

Two weeks of laughing and pottery lessons, dinner and romantic mornings in bed...all irrelevant. They were still exactly where they'd started. Where they'd always been going: nowhere.

She'd known that. But it hadn't mattered. Now, for all her personal pep talks, she wanted more.

Now, she had a choice.

She could walk away—as she'd been trying to do ever since Seb had walked back into her life. It was the obvious decision. The intelligent one. If she had any chance of retaining control over her heart—and the pain that might be inflicted upon it—that was exactly what she should do.

Or she could stay. Which was the wrong decision. The nonsensical one. The one that had her all tangled up and clinging to hopes and dreams that would never materialise. That would lead, inevitably, to rejection. Because Seb would move on—just as Ben had. He would reject her—just as her father had.

But of course it was too late. Because the idea of not seeing Seb again—or even not seeing Seb *tomorrow*—made her heart ache.

She wasn't strong enough to walk away.

She hated that.

'Mila?'

Calmly, she picked up the bowl of glaze again and settled herself back on her stool. She looked up at Seb and smiled. And it was genuine—even after all that just looking at him made her heart sing. It was infuriating, but it was also reality.

'Should we get back to glazing your pot?'

She could see the disquiet in his gaze. Reality had intruded. Mila could no longer pretend that what they had was anything but temporary.

Seb had never wavered from thinking it was. That was obvious. And she'd made her choice. For however long this lasted.

But Seb had a choice, too. The perfect bubble surrounding their idyllic not-a-relationship had been destroyed with awkward questions and incomplete answers. Was this still what Seb wanted? Would he walk away? The way Mila couldn't?

The legs of Seb's stool scraped loudly on the floor as he dragged it beside Mila's.

'Teach me everything you know about glazes,' he said.

Mila laughed out loud. 'That could take a while.'

And so—for now, at least—it seemed Seb had made his choice, too.

CHAPTER FOURTEEN

MILA STOOD IN front of Seb's bathroom mirror. She'd stayed over last night. They'd made their own pizza and talked about their days. It had all seemed pretty normal—really no different from any other evening over the past few weeks.

Except Seb hadn't stayed over at *her* place the night before—the night of their disastrous discussion in her workshop. She hadn't invited him to stay, and he hadn't asked. At the time, some space had seemed like a good idea.

By the next morning she'd missed him. They'd organised to meet up after work—she'd told him she'd make up a batch of pizza dough and bring it over. When he'd called he'd sounded completely normal. She'd sounded normal too, she thought.

She hadn't really *felt* normal, though.

And there was a tension between them now. A tension she really didn't like.

Except when they touched. Or kissed. Or made love. Then—well, then there was still tension. But it was the delicious kind. The kind that made the preceding tension worth ignoring, or at the very least worth forgetting about.

But later—like now, as Mila got ready for work—there was nothing to distract her. To make her forget. Instead it was just obvious that everything had changed.

Seb stepped into the bathroom, his length reflected in the mirror. His gaze caught hers momentarily. He was working on site today, so was in his work clothes, his feet still bare.

His gaze didn't reveal much. Although there wasn't really anything to hide. It was crystal-clear what was going on.

No longer could they blithely carry on as they had before. Now they both knew they wanted different things.

Mila had reflected, of course, on how exactly she'd wanted Seb to answer her question. How she'd wanted Seb to define them.

There was really only one possible answer: she'd wanted Seb to say that she was his girlfriend.

It wasn't something she'd consciously considered. Up until the point when she'd asked Seb she hadn't allowed herself to think like that. Even now the concept felt slightly strange...that she could—theoretically—be Seb's *girlfriend*. It was a foreign label after a lifetime of friendship. But it was also the logical label—because she'd known the moment Ivy had walked in and seen them together that she wanted something more. Even as she had attempted to hide their relationship from her sister, she'd also wanted to flaunt it. And it was that contradiction that had fuelled her frustration, fuelled her need to demand from Seb answers he'd been unprepared to give.

But she couldn't regret asking her questions. No matter how badly Seb's response had hurt her.

With those questions she'd gained knowledge, and with that knowledge, choices. She might not have taken the opportunity to walk away from Seb then, but the option remained.

When it came to the men in her life, in recent memory she hadn't had a heck of a lot of control. It had been *their* choices that had impacted on *her*—while she'd had no choices at all.

So she *would* walk away from Seb—when she was ready. The uncomfortable tension between them meant it would probably be sooner rather than later, and that realisation was a sharp blow to her heart.

Mila brushed her teeth, as did Seb.

He applied sunscreen with a tropical coconut scent to his face, neck and arms as she did her make-up. Their eyes met again in the mirror as Mila applied her mascara.

And just like that the tension shifted. No longer awkward, but luxurious. Warm. *Hot.*

Mila re-capped her mascara calmly, placing it on the marble vanity. Then she turned to face Seb.

His gaze travelled all over her—caressing her legs, hips, waist, breasts...lips.

Mila smiled, then stood on her bare tiptoes to press her mouth against his. And that was that. The kiss was as intense and sexy and amazing and emotional as every kiss they'd ever had.

And later—with reapplied make-up and slightly rumpled clothing—when Mila walked out of the apartment building to her car she knew why she hadn't walked away.

Because not everything had changed between them. The connection between them that pulled them together so intensely had not deviated. It hadn't since that first kiss on the beach.

And that connection was so strong, and so unique—at least to Mila—she wasn't quite pre-pared to let go of it just yet.

A heatwave hit Perth the next day.

Seb stood on the side of the pool, his toes curl-ing over the stone edging.

The diving board was long gone, tossed out during one of his parents' renovations. He missed it right now. He missed the way it would bend beneath his weight. He missed the slightly rough surface beneath the soles of his feet. He missed the satisfying *boing* noise it had made as he'd jumped.

Always one, two, three...*splash!*

But now he remained on the edge of the pool, perfectly dry in his board shorts, enjoying the oppressive blanketing heat against his skin. Even enjoying the way his sweat beaded and dribbled down between his shoulder blades and along the slight trough of his spine.

He'd always liked this—this getting deliciously hot and uncomfortable, knowing that the relief of the water was within his reach. The anticipation was half the fun.

Mila, of course, had always jumped right in. She'd walk through the gate, dump her towel on any available surface and leap into the water straight away. Every time. Every *single* time.

Seb bent his knees and pushed off from the edge of the pool, diving sleekly into the water.

It was so ridiculously hot the water wasn't really even that cold. But it still felt glorious against his skin, washing away the sweat and the heat in an instant.

He surfaced at the far side, where it was shallow enough for him to stand. He turned, propping his back against the warm paving, and looked back across the pool. At the end was the pool house. Empty now, with his parents away on a cruise, the bi-fold doors all closed up.

It was the middle of the afternoon. All day he'd felt restless. The heat, he'd thought—although that had made no sense within his air-conditioned office.

In the end he'd rescheduled his afternoon meetings, deciding some physical exertion might be what he needed. But now he was here he acknowledged it wasn't as simple as finding an outlet for his unease.

If he was honest, the restlessness wasn't even new. It had been hovering for days.

Three days, actually.

Since that afternoon at the workshop.

Seb sank beneath the water, then pushed strongly off the wall with his feet, swimming an expansive breaststroke, under water, to the other side.

Nothing had changed between himself and Mila. At least, not on the surface.

They still saw each other daily. Still shared the same bed.

But things had changed.

Of course they had.

That afternoon had exposed the naiveté of their arrangement. It was all well and good to just go with the flow, and get caught up in the thrill of being 'not just friends'—but it couldn't last for ever. He'd always known that. But he'd been ignoring it.

What had he thought would happen? *Really?*

Had he hoped that after sleeping together for a few weeks he and Mila would magically morph back into 'just friends' again? As if they'd simply needed to get it out of their system?

How stupid. How impossible.

He'd told himself he'd been honest and up-front with Mila. She knew his position on relationships. He'd been crystal-clear.

And he'd been honest that afternoon in the workshop. He'd been unwilling to define their relationship, but he'd told her how he'd felt, how she made him feel.

So he could tell himself that he'd done the right thing. That he was still a good guy.

But he wasn't.

Because when Mila had asked him to define their relationship she'd been telling him that she wanted more. He'd known that—of course he had.

And that had been his cue. His cue to end this—

to walk away before it became even more compli-cated. Before he hurt her even more. And he knew he'd already caused her pain. He'd seen it in her eyes that afternoon.

But he hadn't walked away. In the end he hadn't been able to.

That had been as selfish as his refusal to go along with Mila's silent plea to hide their relation-ship from Ivy.

He'd had no right to react the way he had. But react he had, driven by an unexpected ache—dis-appointment, maybe?—that Mila didn't want the people she cared about to know about them. About the relationship he'd later refused to define.

And here he was—right amidst the tangle of contradictions that was Mila and Seb.

He couldn't give Mila what she wanted. But he also couldn't walk away.

How much longer could this last? How much longer could they continue to fall asleep on Mila's couch? Or to wake up in his bed together covered only in the morning sun? How long before what they had deteriorated? Before what they had be-came so complicated that walking away felt im-possible? And staying together felt unbearable.

How long before their lives became about his-tory and obligation and not...?

Love.

Seb ducked under the water again. He swam as close to the bottom as he could, so that his knees and chest grazed the textured surface. When he reached the end he pushed off again, swimming another underwater lap, and then another—until his body was screaming for oxygen.

When he broke the surface he was gasping for air. He hauled himself out at the side of the pool and rolled immediately onto his back, water streaming from his body to cool the red-hot paving.

He looked up at the sun, right in the middle of the sky, blinding him so that he blinked and squinted.

This wasn't about love.

This was about finally doing the right thing by the women in his life.

He'd let Stephanie down—so badly. He wasn't going to make that mistake again. He just couldn't. He *wouldn't*.

He needed to do the right thing by Mila.

He needed to end it.

As Mila twisted the red and white sign to *'Closed'* two familiar faces walked up to the glass shop door.

April and Ivy.

And Nate, in his pram—invisible beneath a canopy of muslins.

'This is an intervention,' Ivy said in her big sister voice, crystal-clear through the glass.

Mila didn't really want to, but she opened the door. She'd been dodging Ivy's calls, so this was not unexpected. 'I suppose you'd better come in,' she said.

'We should,' April said, deliberately cheerful. 'And, look—I brought doughnuts. Let's go upstairs.'

A few minutes later they were settled with cups of tea at Mila's dining table. Nate sat on an old hand-made quilt that had once been Mila's, sucking happily on a cracker that Ivy had produced from her handbag.

April had carefully sliced each of the different types of glazed doughnut into thirds, so they could all try each flavour. Unexpectedly, that simple, typically April gesture of kindness made Mila's eyes sting and fill with tears.

She blinked them away, annoyed with herself. What was she even upset about? But she wasn't fast enough.

'Oh, honey,' Ivy said, scooting her chair closer so she could wrap her arm around Mila. 'Please tell us what's going on. You had to know you couldn't get away with avoiding us for ever.'

April must have located her box of tissues, because they appeared on the table before her. Mila grabbed a couple, balling them together in her hands.

'I don't know why I'm upset,' she said. 'I don't have anything to be upset about.'

April raised an eyebrow. 'You sure?'

'Yes,' she said. Then, 'No.'

Dammit. She was supposed to be in control. Of what was happening with Seb. Of her emotions.

'If it helps,' Ivy said, 'April and I are confident that Sebastian Fyfe has not suddenly taken an interest in traditional pottery techniques. We've made an educated guess as to what's going on.'

'I'd hoped I was more convincing the other day.'

Ivy laughed. 'Mila, I practically had to fan myself when I walked in the door. *Nate* knew that Seb wasn't there to play with clay.'

Mila raised an eyebrow. 'He actually *is* pretty interested in what I do.'

'I'm sure he is,' said April, with a smile. 'But he's more interested in *you.*'

Mila's cheeks were warm. 'Okay…' she conceded.

'So why the secrecy?' Ivy asked. 'This isn't like you.'

Mila took her time selecting a doughnut piece, and then a bit longer to eat it. Even now her sisters knew something was going on with her and Seb, it was still difficult for her to articulate *what*, exactly.

'Because we're not going out,' Mila said. 'We're just sleeping together. Neither of us saw the point of telling anyone about something so temporary.'

'*Is* it temporary?' asked April.

Mila nodded.

'Is that what you want?' asked Ivy.

She shook her head.

'Ah…' her sisters said, together.

Mila shrugged. 'So that's it. But it's okay. I know what I'm doing.'

After a few moments Ivy said carefully, 'And what's that?'

'Look,' Mila said firmly. 'You really don't have to worry about me. I'll be fine. I'm not being stupid.'

'You're never stupid, Mila!' April said, raising her eyebrows.

Mila rolled her eyes. 'Oh, come on—you both think I'm stupid every time I answer one of Dad's phone calls. And you both thought Ben was a massive loser, long before he cheated on me.'

'Not *stupid*,' April said. 'Impressively optimistic.'

Mila's lips quirked upwards. 'I'm not being optimistic this time. I know Seb isn't desperately in love with me.'

She'd meant it to sound light, like a joke. But it hadn't really come out that way. Instead it had sounded like a statement of fact.

Which she supposed it was.

Oh.

Why did that hurt? As if this was a stunning realisation?

'If he doesn't, then he's the stupid one, Mila,' April said. 'And—'

Ivy interrupted. 'Does he know how you feel about him?'

Mila shook her head. How could he? She didn't really know either. She just knew she wanted more than he was willing to give. 'It doesn't matter.'

'I think it does,' Ivy said, all authoritative.

'No,' Mila said, equally definitely. 'He's made it clear. He doesn't want a relationship with me. It doesn't matter what I say.'

She didn't really want to focus too much on what she felt. It would only make everything that much harder.

And what were the options, anyway? For how she felt? They weren't in high school any more. She couldn't *like* him, like him.

But could she love him?

No.

'It doesn't matter anyway,' Mila said firmly. To herself as much as to her sisters. 'I'm going to end it soon. Before it gets even more complicated.'

'Good idea,' said Ivy.

'What a shame,' April said at the same time. 'It would've been kind of nice to end up with your first love.'

'You *knew*?' Mila said, genuinely stunned. April and Ivy, to the thirteen-year-old Mila, had seemed so much older. It hadn't been until her late teens that she'd started to share her romantic dramas with them both.

'Of course—' began Ivy, but then she was distracted by a thud.

Nate had crawled over to the couch and tugged Ivy's bag to the ground. He happily sat with the strap in his mouth, the detritus from within the bag spread around him—lip balm, tissues, a nappy, Ivy's purse, crumpled receipts…

'Oh, whoops,' Ivy said, getting to her feet. 'I'd better give this to you before I forget. I found it shoved down the side of Nate's pram this morning.'

Ivy came back to the table, handing Mila a slightly chewed package delivery card that Nate had presumably pilfered.

'I'm sorry,' Ivy said. 'It's a few weeks old. Hopefully whatever it is will still be at the post office.'

It was most likely supplies, so Mila wasn't too worried. Instead she focused on the still mostly uneaten doughnuts—and changed the subject. 'So, April,' she said, 'I saw you were making all your followers insanely jealous about a new watch today. New sponsor?'

Mila's phone rang as she was setting up a new window display. The shop was closed, although the sun hadn't quite set—the days were long now, as Christmas approached.

She fished her phone out of the front pocket of her apron, expecting it to be a customer who'd planned to call her back about a commission.

Instead, the number on the screen was international, and Mila's heart sank. She knew it was her father. She recognised the number she'd allowed to go to voicemail only a few weeks earlier. She hadn't listened to his message—only enough to verify that it was Blaine before promptly deleting it.

It had been easy to ignore Blaine then, amongst the drama of that first night with Seb. And it should be equally easy now—but then, he'd never called

240 THE BILLIONAIRE FROM HER PAST

her this regularly before. And it had been unusual for him to attempt to contact her sisters...

She answered the call. She needed to let him know not to contact her again.

'La-la!'

Of course this was the one time her father had called her without the unnecessary help of his assistant. Regardless, she had no qualms about telling him to go away.

'I don't want to talk to you, Blaine.'

'Blaine?'

'Yes,' Mila said. 'I don't want to talk to you, and I don't want you to contact me again.'

Her voice sounded strong, but the words were still so hard to say. She had to force them out, focusing on each word, one after the other.

'But, Mila, I have some wonderful news!'

That didn't matter. She should hang up.

'What, Dad?' she said on a sigh, not quite able to be the ice queen he deserved.

She immediately realised her mistake. *Blaine*—not Dad. *Blaine.* She gritted her teeth, furious.

She was so busy being annoyed with herself, Blaine's words didn't sink in at first.

'Pardon me?' she said, certain she'd heard him wrong. *'Wife?'*

'Didn't you get my message, La-la?' Blaine said,

with a self-satisfied chuckle. 'I got married! To the most amazing woman!'

So it would seem that since she'd last seen him he'd married a woman Mila had never heard of, let alone met. Mila rubbed her temple, just wanting this call to be over.

'But that isn't why I called, of course—because the news is now even better! I wanted *you* to be the first to know, La-la—after my lovely wife and myself. Ha-ha!'

'First to know what?' Mila asked slowly, as horrid realisation began to dawn.

'Can't you guess? I'm going to be a daddy again, La-la! Isn't that amazing? A new brother or sister for you and the girls!'

Oh, God.

'I'm just so excited. I can't—'

But Mila had hung up on him, unable to stomach another word. She squeezed her eyes shut, trying to process the news somehow, to deal with it in a calm and rational manner. Because, really, why did she care what her deadbeat dad was doing on the other side of the world? Why should she care if he was having another child for whom he'd just shown more interest, excitement and affection than Mila had received in *twenty-five years*…?

She turned, needing a glass of water or something. But as she turned her hand clipped one of the tall, elegant vases she'd just put in the shop window. It tipped over, instantly creating a beautiful multi-coloured set of dominoes as each vase smashed its neighbour.

She could probably have saved most of them if she'd reached out and caught one of those subsequent vases. But she hadn't. Instead she'd just stood there, allowing weeks of her work to be destroyed, until she'd found herself sitting cross-legged on the floor, with the remnants of her vases surrounding her and tears streaming down her cheeks.

The shop was empty, new ceilings and fresh plaster now hiding the electrical and plumbing work of the past few weeks.

Seb stood upstairs, standing in the long rectangle of fading light thrown through the street side window. The floors were still raw wood, waiting to be polished. A new kitchen waited to be assembled in the corner, in a collection of beige cardboard boxes.

Seb really liked this part of the building process—when the wooden skeleton was dressed in plasterboard and the interior began to take shape. Although he wasn't really walking around his shop to admire the workmanship of his builders.

He was stalling.

Mila was expecting him in a few minutes. He hadn't seen her since his swim—and his decision—because she'd cancelled their plans for yesterday after being invited out for dinner with her sisters.

He hadn't minded. He didn't mind delaying the inevitable—and he certainly didn't mind delaying hurting Mila.

He still knew it was the right decision. Twenty four hours of over-thinking it hadn't changed a thing.

But still he stalled.

He ran his fingers along the wall. The surface was smooth, but—

A loud crash stopped Seb in his tracks.

The series of crashes that followed had him racing down the stairs, his boots a loud staccato on the bare boards.

Outside, it was now almost dark, but Seb could still make out Mila inside her shop, her pale apron a contrast to the dark wooden floor. He knocked on the shop window and her head jerked upwards, her eyes wide.

'Are you okay?' he asked.

She nodded her head, but Seb was less than convinced.

Behind him, the street light came on, and for a moment—just before Mila glanced away—it revealed a river of tears on her cheeks.

Immediately Seb went to the door—of course it was locked.

'Mila, please let me in.'

She didn't look at him through the glass as she unlocked the door, or as she opened it, or even as he stepped through the doorway. Nor as she turned her back to close the door, and to lock it in a series of clunks and clicks.

But she did when she turned around.

She looked right at him—and then threw herself into his arms.

Mila pressed herself tight against him, wrapping her hands behind his neck and burying her face in his chest. He hugged her tightly—as close as he could.

'Mila, please tell me what's wrong.'

'Would you believe,' she said against the fabric of his T-shirt, 'that this is all because I broke a few vases?'

'No,' Seb said.

'Didn't think so,' she said, her words muffled.

'Do you want to talk about it?'

She lifted her head to meet his gaze. Her tears

had smudged her make-up, so she had dark patches beneath each eye.

'No.' A beat. 'Yes.' She half smiled, then sighed. 'My dad,' she said. 'He called. Let me down—spectacularly this time.'

She'd loosened her hold on Seb, but hadn't made any move to step away.

'What did he do?' Seb asked, his words hard-edged.

'Well!' she said, expansively. 'It's quite a story. But the condensed version is this: my dad called me tonight to tell me he's married a woman I've never heard of and they're having a baby. Isn't that *great*?'

Seb swore harshly.

He hadn't thought it was possible to hate Mila's father more than he already did—but, yes, it clearly was.

'I am *so* sorry, Mila.'

She nodded again—a short, sharp movement. 'Me too,' she said.

She looked at him for a while, exploring his face, as if she was going to say more. Her tears had stopped, but her cheeks were shiny with their remnants.

Eventually, she just smiled. 'I'm starving—should we order dinner?'

He hadn't planned to stay. He'd planned a different conversation entirely. But he couldn't have that conversation now—not after Blaine's phone call.

'Sure,' he said, and followed her up the stairs.

And—while he would do anything to prevent Mila's dad hurting her ever again—he couldn't pretend he was anything but grateful to have more time with Mila.

Mila had fallen asleep on the couch. Her head rested just beside his shoulder, pillowed against the cushions.

He'd barely watched the movie; his concentration had been focused on Mila. Her tears had dried, and she'd laughed when she'd seen the mess of her make-up in her bathroom mirror. Her face was now scrubbed clean, and Seb could just see the tiniest of freckles across the bridge of her nose. He'd seen them before—he now knew every inch of Mila Molyneux's body—but tonight they seemed particularly beautiful. Particularly poignant. Mila always washed her face before bed. So those freckles spoke of early-morning kisses, of sleepy cuddles and of making love before work.

All things he would never get to experience with her again.

Mila blinked and her eyes fluttered open. She

shifted, resting her weight on her hands and leaning, just slightly, towards him. She was exploring his face—her gaze like a touch against the length of his nose, his cheekbones, his jaw, his lips.

'Kiss me,' she said, so softly.

A better man would've refused. It wasn't right, given his decision. But in the end the words he needed to say escaped him.

Her name fell from his lips just before they touched hers, his voice rough and jagged. He didn't kiss her politely. No—he kissed her as if all the reasons he shouldn't no longer existed. As if all that mattered was the part of him that *needed* Mila—needed her mouth and her hands and her freckles. That needed her smile and her wit and her drive.

Her mouth was equally desperate against his, as were her hands—tangled in his hair, shoved beneath his shirt. Hot and needy and frantic.

Now she was on top of him, sitting up to drag her T-shirt off over her head. She was so beautiful. So perfect.

Her skin was heaven beneath his hands and mouth, his skin hot beneath her touch. They both still wore too many clothes, but the narrow couch was making it almost impossible for Seb to move without tipping them both onto the floor.

So instead, in one movement, he stood, scooping Mila up into his arms. She laughed against his neck, then kissed his jaw as he strode towards her room.

'I told you I'd always carry you to bed,' he said.

And with that everything stopped.

Mila went completely still—for a split second. And then she was struggling, pushing against his chest.

'No,' she said.

Immediately he let her go, standing her gently on the floor.

She practically ran from him, searching the small room for her shirt. She kept her back to him as she pulled it over her head—and the contrast of that gesture with its counterpart only minutes ago was as pointed as a blade to Seb's chest.

He had no idea what he'd done wrong. 'What's going on, Mila?'

She shook her head. 'I can't do this any more. You need to go.'

She was right. But... 'I can't.'

'Really?' she said, crossing her arms.

He'd never seen Mila like this before—with such nothingness in her gaze.

'What does that mean? Because I don't have time for empty promises, or for romantic gestures without substance.' She glared at him. '*"I told you I'd always carry you to bed,"*' she mocked. 'Right.'

'I meant that,' he said.

And he had.

None of this was anywhere close to what he'd planned. But he couldn't lie to Mila.

Maybe he could no longer lie to himself.

Mila laughed. 'Save your smooth moves for a woman you actually want to have a relationship with, Seb.'

'But I *do* want to have a relationship with you,' he said, the realisation hitting him as forcefully as a semi-trailer. 'Very much.'

This silenced her. For a moment he thought that maybe it would be okay. That he'd seen a flicker in the flatness of her expression.

'*No,*' she said. 'Not today, Seb. You are *not* going to pretend that you want me—not today.'

'I'm not pretending anything.'

He was standing near the hallway and he stepped towards her, hating being so far away. But she held up her hand, stopping him in his tracks.

'It doesn't matter, anyway,' Mila said. 'I've changed my mind. I don't want to be "not just friends", or your girlfriend, or your *anything* any more.'

'I don't believe you,' he said.

She waved her hand dismissively. 'Don't be so arrogant.'

But he wasn't going to let her do this. Not now.

'I think I've worked it out,' Seb said. 'What happened down in the workshop the other day...why I hated it that you wanted to hide us from Ivy.'

Mila was doing her best to look bored. 'I don't care,' she said.

'When it was you hiding us from Ivy it was all about what *I* wanted—I wanted those close to us to know about us, so I was hurt. But then—when you made it clear that you wanted more than what we had, that you were invested in us...' Mila was determinedly not looking at him, but he couldn't stop. 'Well, then it wasn't just me who could get hurt. And that was the problem—suddenly I held the potential to hurt you in my hands, and I couldn't deal with it.'

His pain didn't matter—he was used to oceans of it—but Mila's? He'd do anything to protect her.

'So you didn't want a relationship with me for my own good?' she said, raising an eyebrow.

'It seemed more noble in my head,' he said.

'And not as condescending?'

'Yes, that too,' he agreed, attempting a small smile.

Mila just narrowed her eyes. But she did move—

striding towards him. She stopped just out of reach, her body radiating emotion.

'So you've decided that you *can* deal with the concept of us going out? Of us telling the world we're together?'

He nodded.

She nodded too, with the slightest of smiles. 'Fine,' she said. 'That's all fine. And I probably would've been happy with that any other day than today. But today that's not enough for me.'

After what had happened with her dad.

'Mila—'

She wasn't listening.

'I shouldn't let him hurt me so much,' she said. 'But I keep on doing it. I've been allowing it for years. Decades. I just keep leaving myself wide open.'

'Mila, it's not your fault—'

'It's taken me too long, but I've finally learned something from all Dad's years of crappy behaviour: I deserve better than that. I deserve to be prioritised and appreciated and *loved*. And I'm not going to accept anything else. From *anyone*.'

Finally Seb began to work out where Mila was headed with this. He met her determined gaze, painfully aware of the beat of his heart in his chest.

'Tell me if I'm going out on a limb, here, but

my guess is that even though you say you want to be my boyfriend, you haven't thought all that far ahead. You're just thinking about the fun stuff: about messing about on the couch, nice dinners, barbecues with friends where you introduce me as your girlfriend. Right?'

Seb didn't move, but Mila knew.

'What about the other stuff? What about in three months' time? In twelve? Are we going to move in together?'

'Mila, I just thought we'd see how things go first—'

'And if we move in together, then what? Are we going to get engaged? Married? Get a dog? Have a kid?'

He shook his head. 'I don't know. You don't know either. We can't know—not yet.'

Seb felt as if he teetered on the edge of a watery abyss, helpless to step anywhere but over the edge.

'Of course not,' Mila said, almost kindly. 'But we *can* know if any of those things are on the agenda. Or even the vaguest possibility.' She paused. 'So—just to be perfectly clear—*are* they on your agenda? With me?'

'This isn't fair, Mila. I lost Steph less than two years ago. The last thing I'm thinking about is getting married again.'

He didn't understand why Mila was doing this.

'I get that—I do,' she said. 'Of course I do. And I'm not expecting a proposal any time soon. But how about the other bits? The house, the dog—you know. The stuff people do when things get serious. When they're committed to each other.'

He hadn't thought about this—about *any* of this. Fifteen minutes ago he'd been working out how he was going to walk away from Mila for ever.

'I don't know what you want me to say.' It was all he could manage, and he knew exactly how pathetic those words were.

'I just need a yes or a no, Seb. It's not difficult.'

But it was. For him and for her. He could see it in her face—could see that slight wobble to her gaze.

There was nowhere else to go—the abyss beckoned. Mila deserved the truth.

'No,' he said. 'No. None of that is on my agenda.'

He just couldn't do it. Ever again. To Mila or to himself.

'With me,' Mila clarified.

'With anyone.'

She shook her head. 'No. With *me*. I'm the only one asking you.'

She wasn't meeting his gaze now. Instead she studied the wall over his shoulder, and the light fittings. The floor.

'You don't understand, Mila, it's not about you—'

'Oh, *God*, Seb—do you hear yourself? Of *course* it's about me. It's *always* about me.'

Her voice cracked, and that just about killed him. But she didn't want to hear anything he said. And he didn't think he could even explain. How could she possibly know the emptiness he was trying to shield her from? Why couldn't she see how great what they already had was? Why ruin it with complications? With plans for the future?

'Why are you doing this, Mila? We've been together for no time at all. How can you possibly know that all those things are what *you* want? After just a few weeks?'

Now she finally came closer. She stood right in front of him, tilting her chin upwards to meet his gaze, her lovely eyes framed with her long naked eyelashes.

'It's not been weeks, Seb. It's been years.'

'Years?'

'Since before you kissed me behind the surf club.'

She closed her eyes and he watched her take a long, deep, breath.

'I've loved you since I was thirteen.' She laughed. 'Just to clarify—then it was hormonal, teenage infatuation. Then later it was platonic—with some effort. But now…'

'Love?' he repeated, shocked to his core.

'Yes,' Mila said. 'Love. It's taken me a while to work it out, but I knew the moment I looked out through my shop window tonight to see you standing outside…I *knew*. I wanted you with me in that moment more than anyone else in the world. I want you with me in most of my moments, actually. And I guess that's love, isn't it?'

Seb had absolutely nothing to say. His brain was desperately attempting to compute what she'd just told him.

'And if I love you then I'm not going to go through the charade of having fun and saying meaningless things about *not being good at relationships*. All that armour is ineffective, anyway— no matter how hard I try. I'm not going to be with you if the only possible outcome is you hurting me. I've had enough of that. I've had enough of allowing that. My dad, Ben. You. I'm done.'

Seb supposed this was the point when he could deny everything that Mila had said. When he could reach across the small distance between them and drag her into his arms—when he could tell her that she was being ridiculous and that he loved her too, that he'd never, ever hurt her…

But none of that would be true.

He loved Mila. He'd loved her for ever. But had it changed from the love of childhood friends? Was he *in* love with her?

It didn't matter, anyway, did it?

Because he knew the second part wasn't true. He knew he couldn't tell her he wouldn't hurt her. He couldn't even tell her that he'd do his best to try not to... Because even that would be a lie.

He *would* hurt her. It was inevitable.

Once he'd loved Steph with all his heart, but he'd still driven her away. To drugs. To her death.

When it came to relationships he was unfixable. And Mila deserved so much more.

'I'm so sorry, Mila,' he said.

Then he left—because he had to.

And deep in his abyss Seb was drowning.

CHAPTER FIFTEEN

STEPH'S BIRTHDAY WAS only a couple of weeks before Christmas.

Mila's pottery classes had finished up a week earlier, but the shop was still incredibly busy, with Sheri and Mila often both needed to manage the constant stream of customers.

With so much demand, and no time to escape to her workshop during the day, Mila had started working late into the night. She'd managed to replace her window display of vases, but she still needed more to maintain a reasonable amount of stock. It was a really good problem to have—although that didn't make Mila any less exhausted.

If she was honest, though, Mila wasn't sure how much sleeping she would've been doing, anyway. Because—unless she was so tired she collapsed into her bed and into oblivion—it was in the darkness that her thoughts would drift to Sebastian.

It made her angry that they did that. It had been

a week now, and she was still wasting her precious time on Seb. Which was pointless.

She'd done the right thing—she knew that. She'd already known she'd needed to walk away, but now she knew exactly why.

It wasn't about avoiding hurt, or rejection.

It was about love.

She deserved love. Nothing less was acceptable.

'Mila?'

Mila had been staring out of the window, her gaze unfocused on the passing traffic.

Sheri grinned. 'You look off with the fairies.'

Mila shook her head, trying to refocus. She'd been leaning against the counter, and now took a step back, running her hands through her curls. 'No, I'm fine.'

'Take the rest of the afternoon off,' Sheri said. '*I'll* be fine.'

The shop was currently empty, but Mila knew it wouldn't last. 'No, I can't do that. It's not fair on you.'

'Staying here isn't fair on *you*,' Sheri said, more softly. 'I know what day it is,' she added. 'I haven't forgotten.'

Mila chewed on her bottom lip, willing the sudden tightness in her throat away.

'If you need an excuse,' Sheri prompted, 'go and

pick up that mystery package. A new delivery card arrived today. It's under the counter.'

By the time Mila had made it to the post office a few days ago, Nate's chewed delivery card in hand, her package had been sent back to the depot to be returned to the sender. Fortunately that hadn't yet happened, and the package had been directed back to Mila.

So she did have a reason to head out.

And, more importantly, Sheri was right. The shop wasn't where she needed to be.

Mila drove to the post office, only a few blocks away. The queue was short inside, and she was handed her package within a few minutes of arriving.

She flipped the large flat box over, curious to note the sender. She and Sheri hadn't been able to work it out—all their outstanding orders had already arrived.

But the handwritten name on the back made Mila go completely still.

'Can I help you with anything else today, miss?' the young man behind the counter prompted politely.

Mila just shook her head furiously and walked briskly to her car. And then she drove to the park.

To the park near the street where she'd grown up, with that giant ancient fig.

Car parked, and the package carefully cradled in her arms, Mila walked towards the towering tree.

The fig's canopy was incredibly dense, stretching out so far that the grass ended some distance from its trunk, unable to grow in the heavy shade. The trunk was huge, with ropey root tentacles that stretched from its centre, large enough to sit upon and stare out across the park.

She chose a spot where she could lean against the base of the fig, and kicked off her flip flops so she could drag her toes in the dirt. She traced the sharp cardboard edges of her package, but didn't move to open it.

She hadn't recognised the sender's writing, but she'd certainly recognised the name. Steph's mum. With a new address from the most southern point of Western Australia, a day's drive from Perth.

Still, she didn't open it.

She'd come here so often with Steph. Exactly here, beneath this tree. This had been *their* place— a place where they'd met without Seb. They'd dreamed up elaborate stories for the fairies they'd imagined lived in the tree, they'd swapped home-work answers, and they'd giggled about boys. They'd made plans for the future: envisaging horse-drawn carriages at their weddings to British princes—one each—the dresses they'd wear to their Year Twelve ball, and which boy they'd like to be the first to kiss them.

They'd been so close. Picture-book best friends.

And then Seb had kissed her.

She'd been thirteen, and the three of them had headed to the beach during the summer holidays. Mila didn't remember many of the details of the day—but she did remember her surprise when she'd realised *Seb was actually going to kiss her.* She'd had a crush on him for ever, but had never done anything about it. She hadn't known what to read into those times when Seb's gaze had tangled with hers, or what to do with the way she'd felt if they as much as bumped shoulders.

She also hadn't really known what to do when his lips had touched hers that first time. Maybe he hadn't either. Either way, it had been a little awkward—and she'd been so embarrassed that she wasn't better at this whole kissing thing. As soon as she'd been able to she'd scampered away—desperate to tell Steph and for her advice. After all, Steph had kissed *two* boys. She had experience.

Steph had been excited for Mila, and even a little jealous—she'd had a bit of a crush on Seb, too. They'd giggled, and planned Mila's next move—but in the end there hadn't been one. Seb had seemed to lose his nerve, and Mila had been so busy trying to play it cool that she'd ended up being snarky and stand-offish.

Mila remembered the day Steph had told her that Seb had kissed *her*. Steph had felt terrible, promising that it would never, ever happen again. Mila had been shattered. But she'd given her blessing. Maybe she'd always thought that Seb falling for her more flirtatious, more vivacious friend was inevitable. Maybe she'd never really believed that Seb could actually want to be with Mila.

And there it was—perfectly encapsulated. The impact she'd allowed her father to have on her self-worth. At thirteen, at almost thirty, and a million times in between.

How could she not have seen it before now?

Mila looked at her toes, her fire-engine-red toenails now dusted with dirt. A short distance away two small boys had appeared, tossing a Frisbee between them. A breeze ruffled the old fig's many leaves.

Mila *knew*. She knew why nothing had been clear until that night when her dad had called her with news of her future half-sibling. Up until that night Mila had held on to a skerrick of faith that somewhere deep down her father *did* love her. But he didn't. He didn't love her. He didn't care about her. He didn't even know her.

And in amongst the devastation of that realisation, there was freedom. No longer would she waste her love on those who didn't deserve it. And no longer would she wait so patiently for love that would never come her way.

She loved Seb. She knew that now. She'd loved him for ever. In different ways, but unwaveringly. She couldn't just switch that off, and—unlike her thirteen-year-old self—she couldn't pretend it wasn't happening.

But at least this time she'd told him about it.

How might her life have been different if she hadn't run away when Seb had kissed her? Although to suggest it would've been different was a disservice to Steph, and to Seb.

For all the problems that Seb had said they'd had towards the end of their marriage, Mila couldn't wish away Steph and Seb's relationship. For a long time they had been incredibly happy together. Mila knew that—she'd been best friend to them *both*.

Steph and Seb had fitted together perfectly—for a long time. They'd had silly inside jokes, and Seb had used to have a really sweet way of tucking Steph's long, wild hair behind her ears. It had been almost reverent, as if he couldn't quite believe he was allowed to touch such beauty.

As a threesome, they'd just *worked*, too. They'd laughed and partied and travelled—it had been fantastic. Maybe she'd been envious of their happiness, but she'd never coveted Seb. Seb and Steph had just gone together. They'd been *meant* to be together.

Mila wondered—just a little—what would've happened if that night in her flat had ended differently. If Seb had said he loved her too. Would she still have wondered, somewhere deep inside, if she was some sort of consolation prize? If she could ever match up to Steph's memory?

A clattering noise grabbed Mila's attention. A bright yellow Frisbee lay only a few metres from Mila's feet, on top of one of the fig's huge roots. One of the small boys had run up to retrieve it, but had stopped dead on seeing Mila in the shadows, suddenly shy.

'It's okay,' Mila said, getting to her feet, placing her package carefully on a wide, shelf-like root 'I'll get it.'

She picked up the Frisbee and tossed it, reasonably impressed with her rusty Frisbee-throwing technique. The boy ran off to his friend and Mila walked the few steps back to her preferred location at the base of the tree trunk.

The sun had lowered further in the sky, illuminating different parts of the tree and its roots as light dodged through the branches. The package—with its plain brown cardboard wrapping and its small stash of colourful stamps—lay in a narrow strip of sunlight, waiting for her.

Mila felt somewhat as she did at the end of a fabulous book—desperate to know the ending, but also hating how few pages remained. Because this package, she knew, had no sequel.

It was from Steph.

How many times had she wished to see Steph just one more time? To talk to her? To hug her? This package—whatever it might be—was as close to granting her wish as she was ever going to get.

Finally she picked the package up and settled back into her seat against the tree. Then quickly—as fast as she could in the end—she tore off the packing tape and prised the box open with trembling fingers.

Inside lay a letter, on top of some fabric wrapped in purple tissue paper.

Dear Mila,
I'm not sure if you knew, but Steph was working on a new collection before she died. With the help of some of her old colleagues we're

releasing one final Violet collection, with all profits to go to charity.

Most of her designs were still at an early design stage—including this dress. But this was the only piece she'd named, so I thought it was important I sent it to you. After all, it's named after you.

I've enclosed the sketches, as I thought you might like to read Steph's notes...

Mila barely read the rest of the letter, her vision blurry with unshed tears. Instead she carefully unwrapped the dress and held it up before her. It was simple—made of a structured, slightly heavy fabric that would reach to mid-knee. It had a boat neck and a flared skirt that would move and swish as she walked. And it was red—lipstick-red, fire-engine-red. Her favourite colour.

It was beautiful.

Carefully, she laid it back in the box and retrieved the small, thin pile of fashion sketches. Drawn in skinny black ink, the willowy model in the sketches bore no resemblance to Mila. But beside the posing, pouting figure were Steph's notes under a simple heading: *Mila.*

And there Steph had listed all manner of words.

Funny.
Determined.
Talented.
Wise.

Mila blinked.

Good listener.
Reliable.
Creative.
Gorgeous.
Loyal.
My best friend.

Underneath, in capital letters, Steph had written: *HOW DO I PUT ALL THAT IN A DRESS?*

Mila squeezed her eyes shut, but it didn't make any difference. Tears fell down her cheeks, splashing onto her jeans.

She'd spent a lot of time over the past eighteen months berating and hating herself for the way her friendship with Steph had changed. For the first time she wondered if she'd been wrong.

Steph van Berlo and Mila Molyneux had been best friends from the age of four—through playgroup, school, university and beyond. Almost all their lives they'd been there for each other. Side by side.

So maybe—*maybe*—it was unavoidable that their lives had diverged. Maybe they'd needed space to grow up without each other—to stand on their own two feet. To be their own people, to be their own women.

And that had been okay, because Mila had known that one day they would come back together. In Perth, or London, or Paris, or San Francisco. Who cared? It hadn't mattered.

But that day had been supposed to come. The day when they would be Mila and Steph again. Just like the inscriptions on those cheap gold-plated pendants they'd bought each other in Year Five: *Friends For Ever.*

It wasn't fair.

Steph's whole life had been ahead of her.

As had a lifetime of friendship.

Mila missed her.

So much.

She stood up, turning her back to the tree, the sketches hugged carefully against her heart.

Mila still harboured a small mountain of regret. She wished she'd never fallen out of the habit of telling Steph about every vaguely exciting event in her life. She wished, desperately, that she'd sent those emails she'd kept forgetting to write. Made those phone calls planned with the best of intentions.

But now—thanks to a beautiful dress and some scribbly sketches—Mila realised that all of that had done nothing to minimise their friendship.

Their friendship *had* changed. It had been reshaped, repositioned. But it had endured—and, given time, it would have been reinvented.

And now Mila knew for sure that Steph had known that too.

The two kids and their Frisbee had left, and the park was now empty again.

'I love you, Steph,' Mila said to the park, to the tree and to the sky.

And Mila knew, more certainly than anything else in her life, that Steph had loved her too.

Seb had taken the afternoon off work to head to Cottesloe Beach.

Steph had loved this beach. Most people in Perth loved this beach. And today that was evident in the sheer number of people absolutely everywhere: inside the bars and restaurants along Marine Parade, walking along the street, scattered across the pure white sand and within the crashing waves.

This was where Seb—along with Steph's parents—had released Steph's ashes. So it was the obvious place to come if he wanted to feel close to Steph. And today he did—on her birthday. Twenty-nine today.

Happy Birthday, Stephanie.

Seb navigated the patchwork of towels and bodies on the sand to find a space for himself. He laid out his towel, then sat, his forearms resting on his bent knees, gazing out to the ocean.

I've mucked things up, haven't I, Steph?

With Steph, and now with Mila.

They'd had so much fun out here, the three of them. They'd used to catch the bus, sharing one big beach bag, stuffed with towels and sunscreen. Seb had always been lumped with carrying it—not that he'd really minded.

It had never quite seemed right that a rather nerdy, weedy, computer-obsessed guy got to spend so much time with such beautiful girls. But as soon as they'd all got old enough to start noticing each other beyond who was hogging all the Play Dough it had always been Mila Seb had been drawn to...

'You are so full of it, Seb!' Mila said, turning on her heel. 'You didn't hear the ice cream van. What a waste of time.'

Seb stepped in front of her, delaying her stalk from the surf club and back to the beach. 'Just wait a sec.'

'Why?' She crossed her arms in front of herself.
She was wearing the two-piece bathers she'd got
for Christmas—red with lime green polka dots.
Her skin was a lovely olive tan, her hair wet and
slicked back after a morning of body-boarding in
the ocean.

'I want to talk to you,' he said.

Mila's eyes narrowed. Her gaze flicked over
him—his bare chest, board shorts and bare feet—
as if searching for whatever she thought he was
hiding.

'Okay,' she said. 'Talk to me.'

But he hadn't really planned what to say. 'It's a
nice day, isn't it?'

Really? Surely he could do better than that.

Mila rolled her eyes. 'Steph is going to be annoyed we didn't get any ice-cream.' She went to
walk away.

'I like your bikini,' he blurted out. 'It matches
your eyes.'

She went still, her gaze dropping to her feet. 'My
eyes aren't red,' she said. 'Or green.'

'I meant...' he said, scrambling. 'I meant they
complement them. Or something.'

Mila looked up, squinting a little in the bright
sun. 'Thank you,' she said.

For a long moment she met Seb's gaze.

What did he do now?

He took too long.

'Well—' Mila began.

But in a rush of panic—or adrenalin, or hormones—he seized the moment.

Seized Mila, really.

He gripped her arms, just lightly, and bent his head towards her.

She blinked and looked stunned. But then she smiled—just a little—and that was all the encouragement he needed.

Her lips were soft and tasted of the ocean. He'd never kissed a girl before, so he didn't really do anything else but press his lips to hers, while his mind madly ran in circles, wondering if he should do something with his tongue.

Worried he was doing it wrong, he ended the kiss. He stepped back, releasing Mila from his grasp.

She lifted her hand and touched her lips.

Seb couldn't work out her expression. Had she liked the kiss? Had he done it right?

'I need to go,' she said, very suddenly.

Then she skirted around him and ran away—back to Steph and their towels...

He hadn't thought about that day in sixteen years.

He'd been so embarrassed, and her rejection had stung. He'd read it all wrong.

He'd been so sure—until that kiss—that Mila had liked him. And, from what Mila had said a few nights ago, she *had*. But he'd been oblivious.

What would've happened if he'd known? Would he have ended up with Mila instead?

And did that mean that Steph wouldn't have moved to London with him, fallen in with the wrong crowd, and died?

He'd been staring out at the waves but now he lowered his head, burying it against his knees.

He been through this in the months after Steph's death. He'd blamed himself a million ways—and now he'd found yet another. If he hadn't been so stupid to not realise Mila loved him...

No.

He couldn't do this. He'd dealt with this.

I'm sorry, Steph. For being a crappy husband. For not being there for you. But not for loving you. Not for marrying you.

He hadn't bought the drugs.

Steph had done that. Steph had chosen to take them.

'Steph's choices are not your responsibility.'

He hadn't believed Mila when she'd said that.

He hadn't been ready to believe it. But these past few weeks something had shifted...

When he was with Mila there was a lightness to his life. A rightness. There was laughter, and silliness, and rambling conversations and *connection*. A connection to the present—to living every day to the best of his ability. A connection to Mila— intimacy, trust, passion. And a connection to his future...

And that was what had scared him.

The future was what had made him walk away. Because in the future things could go wrong. *Very* wrong. He could make mistakes. He could ruin everything. He could hurt Mila.

'Steph's choices are not your responsibility.'

He believed that now.

He did.

Her death hadn't been his fault.

As if you could make *me do anything!*

He could almost hear Steph's voice, and her laughter, caught up in the ocean breeze.

It wasn't his fault.

He'd told himself this a hundred times, and for the first time it seemed to sink in. For the first time he realised he believed it.

It wasn't his fault.

'Steph's choices are not your responsibility.'

They were hers.

And he sat there alone, on a beach full of memories, without the two women most important to him.

Because of Steph's choices.

And because of his.

The only reason Mila was not sitting beside him, right this second, was because of his own choices. His own decisions.

He was responsible for that.

Seb lifted his head from his knees as a seagull landed at his feet, pecking hopefully at his towel for food. Around him the beach practically heaved with activity and colour—with *life*.

Why wasn't Mila here with him? Sharing this with him?

Because he didn't want to hurt her. He didn't want their relationship to deteriorate as his relationship with Steph had.

But...

He didn't shirk from the role he'd played in his marriage falling apart. In fact he embraced it. He knew he was responsible for the mistakes he'd made. For the choices he'd made...

And of course that was it. *He* was responsible for his choices. Just as Steph had been for hers. Just as Mila was.

And Mila—unbelievably, amazingly—had chosen *him*. She'd chosen Sebastian Fyfe, with all his flaws and messy emotions.

And Seb—*he'd* chosen to run away from a Technicolor future with Mila. Out of fear.

Fear that when it came to relationships he was broken. Unfixable. That a relationship with Mila would inevitably lead to hurt and to pain. That he'd make the same mistakes as before.

As if he was just some helpless pawn in his own life, predestined to follow exactly the same path.

His ridiculous. How stupid.

He was responsible for his future. *He* was responsible for his choices—in life and in his relationship with Mila. He was responsible for learning from his mistakes.

So Mila had chosen Seb—despite the pain of her past, despite everything. Despite probably knowing that he was so caught up in his past that he'd reject her. She'd chosen courage.

While Seb had chosen fear.

That ended now.

CHAPTER SIXTEEN

THE NEXT DAY was Saturday. It had been *crazy* busy at Mila's Nest—the busiest day Mila had ever had. She'd even sat down and worked that out on her laptop. Online sales were through the roof, too—in fact she'd needed to close for new orders as she just couldn't keep up with demand.

Next year she'd need to work something out—maybe make some slip cast moulds, or even look into getting some of her designs commercially produced. The prospect was both exciting and a little sad—it felt like the end of an era. No longer would everything she sold be made with her own hands.

But tonight she was definitely using her own hands. She sat at her potter's wheel, the radio humming in the background, wet clay beneath her fingertips.

She was completely absorbed in her creation—gently manipulating the clay from featureless lump into an elegant, elongated vase—when there was a knock at the workshop door.

It was a warm December evening, so she'd left the door open. Only the security screen separated Mila from her visitor, and it rattled under the definite tap of Seb's knuckles.

'Hey,' he said.

Not sure what to do with Seb's unexpected appearance, Mila momentarily lost her focus—and under her wayward fingers the vase collapsed.

'Dammit!' She brought the wheel to a stop.

Seb swore. 'Sorry—I didn't mean—'

'I'm a bit busy at the moment,' Mila interrupted, as she patted the ruined vase back into a lump. 'Please leave.'

That had been incredibly hard to say—which Mila didn't like.

She kept her gaze downwards as she slapped a new mound of clay onto the wheel head, then dipped her fingers into the adjacent bowl of water so she could dampen the clay.

'I'm not going anywhere,' he said.

Mila closed her eyes. 'It's a lovely night,' she said. 'There are thousands of better things you could be doing than watching me work.'

'I can't think of any.'

Mila shook her head. No, he didn't get to be charming.

She stood up and went to the sink to wash her

hands, her back to Seb. She dried her hands on her apron, twisting her fingers in the fabric.

Why didn't this get easier? It had been a week. Shouldn't it not hurt so much by now? But instead Mila felt as raw as when he'd told her no.

He didn't want her. Why was he here?

She took a deep breath before turning and walking to the door. He looked as handsome as always—in a dark grey T-shirt and black board shorts—his shoulders broad, his calves muscular.

Maybe Seb had thought she was going to let him in—but he rapidly realised his mistake as she reached for the heavy workshop door.

'Wait, Mila,' he said. 'Please let me in.'

She shook her head again.

No, no, no.

'You know,' she said, quite conversationally from her side of the fly screen, 'I was thinking about Steph yesterday.'

She didn't need to clarify why.

He nodded. Of course he had been, too.

'I was thinking about how much I miss her. How I'd love to hear her laugh just one more time.' She took a deep breath. 'And then I started wondering what would have happened if you and I *had* started going out. If the other night you'd said yes instead of no.'

'Mila—'

'And I thought…I wonder if he would've compared me to Steph? And if he did how would I have stacked up? Would I have been just the substitute, or the consolation prize, or simply his second choice?'

Seb was furious. 'Let me in, Mila. You are—'

'But then,' Mila said, 'I realised I was being an idiot.'

Seb went still.

'Because when I'm with you…' A pause. 'When I *was* with you, you never made me feel like that. You never made me feel like anything but the focus of your attention. When I was with you, you made me feel like the centre of your universe. You made me feel special, and treasured, and *valued.* Just for being me, nothing more.' She swallowed. 'I haven't felt like that before. I've never felt like someone's most important person. I liked it. I loved it, really.'

He was letting her talk now.

'I'm sorry it's over, but that's okay. I'm okay— really. You didn't need to check up on me, or whatever it is you're doing. Thank you for making me feel like that, and for helping me realise that I want that feeling again. That I deserve to feel like that.' Another long pause. 'But I don't want to see you again, Seb. It's too hard.'

She reached for the door, needing to close it quickly, so she no longer had to look at Sebastian.

'Let me in, Mila—please.'

She shook her head silently and gripped the door handle.

'Dammit, Mila, I don't want to say this through a fly screen. Let me in.'

There was nothing he could possibly say. She swung the door shut.

Seb spoke again, a split second before the door clicked shut.

'I love you, Mila!'

But the door was closed.

'I love you!'

He was shouting. She could hear him clearly through the door. She should walk away—he'd only clarify those words if she let him in: he loved her *as a friend*.

But when it came to Sebastian Fyfe, as always, she was weak. She opened the door, but not the security screen.

'I love you,' he said again. 'You *are* my most important person.'

'And you don't want to lose our friendship—blah-blah-blah. Haven't we been through this before? It's kind of old.'

'*No,*' he said. 'I've been an idiot. Please hear me out.'

She nodded, but sharply. 'Be quick. I have a vase to make.'

Mila crossed her arms, refusing to be anything but sceptical.

'I loved Steph,' he said. 'You know that. We loved each other like people do in books and movies, I thought it was perfect. I thought our relationship was perfect. But then we got married, we moved overseas, our businesses took off...and everything changed. I don't really know if it changed fast or slow—but one day our relationship had broken and it never stopped breaking. Our marriage was over in every way but officially. We were done.'

He stood there, on the other side of the security screen, watching Mila with a measured intensity.

'And that was the thing. Steph and I started with so much and ended up with nothing. *Worse* than nothing, actually. It was like we'd created a vacuum between us, which swallowed up all our hopes and plans for a future together and left us each alone in the darkness. It was miserable.' He swallowed. 'I made a lot of mistakes in my marriage. I prioritised my work over Steph. I prioritised my work over everything. And I shoved my head in the sand when it came to Steph and I. I hurt her—a lot. I hate that I did that. And I was terrified that I'd do that to you.'

Mila had uncrossed her arms, and her fingers were now tangling again in her apron.

'So when you started talking about love the other night I did panic. It's hard for me to believe in love, given what happened in my marriage. It isn't really an emotion that I trust. But mostly I was worried about you. I don't ever want to hurt anyone the way I hurt Steph. I believed I was beyond repair. That loving me meant that hurt was guaranteed. I couldn't do that to you.'

'What's changed?' Mila asked.

Seb nodded. 'You,' he said. 'You've changed me, Mila. You've shown me that I need to leave the past behind. That, while I need to learn from my mistakes, I need to move forward. You told me once about your plans to protect yourself from hurt in relationships—and I know how much you've been hurt in the past. And yet you threw all that away. For *me*. You risked hurt—hurt that you're all too familiar with—for a man you knew was all kinds of messed up and likely to throw it in your face.'

Because I love you—Mila thought. But she was wasn't ready to say it aloud. Not yet.

'Life is all about choices, Mila. I finally get that.

And I promise you right now I choose *not* to be a selfish, distant workaholic ever again.'

Mila's lips quirked upwards, despite the swirling and still uncertain emotion between them.

'But I know that I'm not the only one with choices in a relationship. You have them too. And I think maybe it was those choices that I was most fearful of. What if you choose to hurt me? To walk away from me? To stop loving me?'

Seb's voice was strong, but raw. Mila's heart beat like a drum against her chest…her fingers twisted in knots inside her apron.

'But you know what? I can't control your choices. I can't control anything but my own. And, as scary as that is for me to realise, I've decided to run with it. To be—for the first time in way too long—truly, properly brave.'

He swallowed, his gaze exploring her face.

'So, Mila—I choose *you*. I choose to love you. I love you, Mila Molyneux, and that won't change—whatever you decide. Whatever you choose. I came here tonight because I thought you deserved to hear that—but also because I needed to say it.' A long, long pause. 'I came here with no expectations. I *will* leave, with no regrets and no bad feelings—I promise—if you don't want me. If you don't love me. If you don't choose—'

'Oh, *God*, Seb, shut up!' Mila said with laughter—and with love. 'Of *course* I choose you!'

With rapid, desperate movements, Mila opened the security screen. Instantly she was in Seb's arms and his lips were at her neck, her jaw, her mouth.

Her hands threaded through his hair. 'I love you,' Mila said softly against his lips.

'I love you, too, Mila,' he said, his lips against her ear, his breath hot against her skin. 'I've loved you since I was fourteen—in a million different ways. But the way I love you *now* is my favourite.'

'This *is* pretty good,' she teased, and then squealed as he lifted her into his arms.

'Can that vase wait?' Seb asked, nodding in the direction of the forgotten pottery wheel.

'That had better not be a serious question,' Mila replied, her mouth against his neck, her laughter only slightly muffled against his skin.

'Of course not,' Seb said, and he practically leapt up the stairs, putting his months of physical labour—Mila thought—to very good use.

At the top of the stairs, he paused. It was dark in Mila's apartment, lit only by the glow of the streetlight and a hint of the moon. But still, in the almost darkness, their gazes met and locked.

Seb was waiting, Mila realised.

Then she smiled.

'Carry me to bed,' she said, so softly.

'Every night?' he asked.

She nodded. 'For ever, please.'

* * * * *

MILLS & BOON®
Large Print – January 2017

To Blackmail a Di Sione
Rachael Thomas

A Ring for Vincenzo's Heir
Jennie Lucas

Demetriou Demands His Child
Kate Hewitt

Trapped by Vialli's Vows
Chantelle Shaw

The Sheikh's Baby Scandal
Carol Marinelli

Defying the Billionaire's Command
Michelle Conder

The Secret Beneath the Veil
Dani Collins

Stepping into the Prince's World
Marion Lennox

Unveiling the Bridesmaid
Jessica Gilmore

The CEO's Surprise Family
Teresa Carpenter

The Billionaire from Her Past
Leah Ashton

MILLS & BOON®
Large Print – February 2017

The Return of the Di Sione Wife
Caitlin Crews

Baby of His Revenge
Jennie Lucas

The Spaniard's Pregnant Bride
Maisey Yates

A Cinderella for the Greek
Julia James

Married for the Tycoon's Empire
Abby Green

Indebted to Moreno
Kate Walker

A Deal with Alejandro
Maya Blake

A Mistletoe Kiss with the Boss
Susan Meier

A Countess for Christmas
Christy McKellen

Her Festive Baby Bombshell
Jennifer Faye

The Unexpected Holiday Gift
Sophie Pembroke